'A nice home you have,' Robert commented as she led him upstairs to the first-floor sitting-room. She took off her jacket and watched him warily as he stepped towards the window. 'A river view; very pleasant.'

'It's...it's even better from the bedrooms upstairs.' Liza could have bitten her tongue out for that. Heat scorched her neck as lazily he turned to her and, with a sardonic smile creasing across his jawline, he said, 'Thanks for the offer but I came here to talk business, not to make love to you.'

'I...I didn't mean that!' she blurted self-consciously. Oh, he was quick, too sharp and suggestive by far.

'Didn't you?' He slid out of his suit jacket, flung it carelessly across her chintz Laura Ashley sofa. 'You wouldn't be the first woman to offer me her body within fifteen minutes of our relationship.'

RELUCTANT MISTRESS

BY

NATALIE FOX

MILLS & BOON LIMITED
ETON HOUSE   18-24 PARADISE ROAD
RICHMOND   SURREY   TW9 1SR

*First published in Great Britain 1991
by Mills & Boon Limited*

© Natalie Fox 1991

*Australian copyright 1991
Philippine copyright 1991
This edition 1991*

ISBN 0 263 77362 0

*Set in Times Roman 11½ on 12 pt.
01-9112-44343 C*

Made and printed in Great Britain

CHAPTER ONE

ROBERT BUCHANAN was everything she had expected him to be. Cool, aloof and as arrogant as the media proclaimed.

Liza observed him through the glass panel of her office, her green eyes calculating every move he made as he toured the editorial offices with John Standish, the editor of *Leisure Days* magazine.

Standish was sweating. Buchanan the cause. With a deep sigh Liza turned away from the sickening scene of the staff flapping and trying to court favour with the new owner, the all-powerful Buchanan, whose reputation for pulping magazines like theirs into sawdust went before him like a flagship of destruction.

They were all scared, including Liza. As advertising director she knew she had nothing to fear as far as her work was concerned, but she had reluctantly to admit that lately it had become more and more difficult persuading advertisers to take space in the magazine. She had succeeded because she was skilled at her job, but how long would it last with Standish taking such an outdated stand on the editorial side? And what were Robert Buchanan's plans for their future? He was fast becoming Europe's top publisher, scooping up ailing periodicals and mutating them till they became clones. All the same, just in a different language.

'Whose head will be the first to roll?' Liza's assistant Julia muttered ruefully from her desk.

Unconciously rubbing her neck, Liza stared bleakly out of the window. 'Whose indeed?' was all she could offer in consolation.

'Do you believe all they say about him in the papers?' Julia asked, her bright eyes looking decidedly interested.

Liza turned to her and smiled, knowing the tangent her man-mad assistant's mind was veering off at. 'Well, there's no smoke without fire, Julia,' she teased. 'Flash your eyes at him the way you do at most men and you just might save your job.'

With a snort Julia tapped away at her computer. 'Would that it were that easy. It's always redheads with him, isn't it? Perhaps I should whisk to the hairdresser's lunchtime and swap my mouse-brown mop for Titian gold like yours.'

'Are you implying mine comes from a bottle?'

'Of course not!' Julia laughed. 'But seriously, he's always being photographed with some gorgeous redhead. You'd better watch out, Liza...' She stopped in mid-sentence as the door opened and the Buchanan entourage stepped into Liza's office.

Julia stumbled to her feet, flushed, and pulled at her sweater nervously. Liza stood where she was, coldly unemotional, her hair brightened to flame by the light from the window behind her. If she had consciously stage-managed her impact on Robert Buchanan she couldn't have done it more successfully. His dark penetrating eyes devoured her from head to toe, and came to rest on the aureole of marmalade frizz that cascaded around her shoulders.

It was easy to give Robert Buchanan a wide smile of welcome, easy to lift her hand and hold it out to him as John stammered out his introductions. Handsome he might be, powerful in publishing he undoubtedly was, but he wasn't a gift from the gods as most women thought. He was a man like any other: ruthless, cold, a taker, just like another she knew.

He even resembled her former lover. He had the same jet hair as Graham, the same tall muscular build. They shared the same characteristics too, if all the papers said about the publishing giant was true: cold, calculating and a heartbreaker where women were concerned. But, whereas Robert Buchanan had maintained his bachelor existence, Graham had fallen prey—to her own sister of all people. They'd been married a year now, a year in which the pain of betrayal was still edged with a sharpness that cut into Liza's very soul at the thought of the two of them, cosily cocooned in their Welsh cottage. Yvonne happily baking and housekeeping while Graham's literary prowess prospered as it never had all the two years they had been lovers.

'So, you are Liza Kay, without whose advertising sales skill this dreary magazine would have bitten the dust months ago.'

His brutal words, so softly, yet deeply, delivered with the faintest of a Scots burr, stunned everyone in the room. There was a long silence, followed by the uneasy shuffling of feet. Poor John looked waxy and gaunt. Liza held her smile with all the loyalty to John she could muster.

'If that was a compliment, Mr Buchanan, I relinquish it on the grounds of bad taste.' She withdrew her hand from his, yet maintained her sweet smile.

He raised a dark brow, that was all, turned from her, and left the office, his minions following, flustered and apologetic.

To Liza's surprise she experienced a tremor through her body, a peculiar *frisson* she couldn't explain away. Slumping down on to her chair, she murmured, 'That was dumb, really dumb!'

'You can say that again!' Julia breathed with a mixture of admiration and awe. 'You'll be the first to go.'

Composed now, Liza scooped her hair back from her face. 'First or last—makes no difference; we're all for the slush pile if Buchanan runs true to form.'

'Don't you care?' Julia quizzed anxiously.

'Of course I care,' Liza admitted on a sigh. 'I've got as big outgoings as the next person.'

'So why insult him in front of everyone like that? You've got to be out of your mind!'

How very right, Liza mused, very regretful now. She had been stupid, incredibly so. If she lost her position, which she undoubtedly would now, what then? Her mortgage was high, taken out when times with Graham had been good and she had hoped he would ask her to marry him. The terraced town house would have been perfect for the two of them. Close to town on the south side of the Embankment, in an up and coming area of Battersea, it was within easy striking distance of the West End. Theatres, restaurants, art exhibitions—everything she had wanted to share with Graham had been at hand, and yet he had chosen to end their relationship for her countrified sister and that hideous cottage in the hills!

That was the root of her insult to Robert Buchanan, she realised with a plop of her heart. She was getting back at Graham, through any man that crossed her path. Buchanan had been the target for the day. Pity she hadn't challenged her insult in the direction of someone less influential. For a twenty-eight-year-old advertising director she *was* pretty dumb!

'I'm sorry,' Liza moaned later when Julia had skipped off to lunch and John Standish sloped into her office. His colour had returned, an infusion brought on by the exit of Robert Buchanan and his henchmen. He slumped in Julia's seat, and rubbed his fevered brow.

'Thanks for your loyalty, but you did yourself no favours, Liza. He stormed out of here like an enraged bull.'

'What's going to happen?'

'He didn't say; ranted on about dropping sales and restructuring the whole set-up, and we both know what that means. New editor for starters.'

Liza opened her mouth to protest but snapped it shut when John raised his hand. 'Don't say anything, Liza. I've brought it on myself. Not moved with the times, have I? He was right, you know. If it weren't for you and your persuasive ways with the advertisers we would have sunk into oblivion a long while back.' He stood up, stretched his long limbs lazily. 'Can I buy you a liquid lunch to drown our sorrows?'

Liza shook her head. 'I've some calls to make. Robert Buchanan hasn't folded us yet. Life goes on.' She reached for the phone, pausing to watch John leave her office. Those liquid lunches didn't help him one bit. Half the afternoon he was in a hazy stupor. His secretary and a variety of assistants had carried him for months now. It was no wonder the magazine was slipping.

Impatiently Liza slammed down the phone. The calls would have to wait: she needed air. Slipping a ginger suede jacket over her dark green suit, she headed for the lift. A brisk walk down Berwick Street Market would clear her head.

February greyness greeted her as she emerged out into Beak Street, but it hadn't put off the tourists in Carnaby Street. They swarmed like excited bees, shrieking with laughter at some of the absurdities for sale. Liza crossed the road, headed in the opposite direction, and was nearly winded as a car door jerked open in front of her. She was about to slam it shut with a suitable expletive when she recognised the back-seat occupant.

'Get in!' Robert Buchanan ordered flintily.

'I'm sorry, I have a lunch appointment,' she lied.

'Yes, with me. Get in before I haul you in, and don't bother making a scene; in Soho it's not unusual for women to be picked up in a limousine.'

Flushing furiously, Liza slid in beside him and slammed the door viciously as a protest.

'Thanks for the comparison,' she fired sarcastically. 'You're obviously an experienced kerb crawler!'

'Does nothing but hell-fire and fury ever emerge from that pretty little mouth of yours?' he drawled as the chauffeur pioneered the huge black limousine through seething masses of lunchtimers in the narrow backstreets of Soho.

'When there's reason to I can charm the birds from the trees,' she told him sweetly, her eyes straight ahead.

'I bet you can,' he murmured, and Liza suspected he might be smiling.

'So what is the purpose of this pick-up?' she asked stiffly, sure she was going to be the first sacking from *Leisure Days* magazine.

'Lunch for one thing, business for another. Creda Court, Battersea, Carl,' he directed at the chauffeur.

Swivelling to face him, Liza gasped. 'Creda Court! But that's where I live!'

He looked at her, dark eyes flecked with shards of silver. 'I know. I thought a homely lunch and a chat out of the public eye a good idea; don't you?'

'I don't!' she rasped.

'So you'd rather we conducted our business in a restaurant with the Press breathing down our necks and you making the gossip columns tomorrow morning?'

Green eyes wide with shock, Liza gaped at him. 'Business? Gossip columns? I haven't a clue what you're talking about.'

She gazed blindly out of the window. Of course she knew what he meant about the Press. Every movement he made was recorded and publicised, but then he asked for it all. He did nothing by halves. Take-overs, mergers, women; they were all the same to him—a challenge! The tabloids loved all that macho action-man stuff—it sold papers. And of course he was good-looking, achingly so.

'I don't think my husband would approve of my picking up strange men and bringing them home for lunch,' she offered when he didn't enlarge on her comments.

'A husband, eh? When was the wedding—this morning in your coffee break?'

'What?'

'At the close of business last night you were very much a single lady. Life moves at a great pace in London, I know, but I'd say an overnight courtship is a bit racy, even for me.'

'You...you know I'm single?' Liza stammered uneasily, a coil of apprehension winding inside her.

'I know everything about you, Liza Kay. Twenty-eight years old. Ten years in publishing, seven of those on the advertising side. Born and educated in Hampstead. Parents still live there. One younger sister, married to the writer Graham Bond with whom you had a two-year relationship——'

'How dare you?' Liza exclaimed angrily, her fiery blood rushing to the boil. 'How dare you pry into my private life? Where did you get all this information and, more importantly, why?' Her heart hammered at her ribcage. What on earth was going on here?

'I don't employ trouble. I have a detailed profile on all my key staff.'

'I'm not your key staff!' she retorted. 'You haven't officially taken over yet. I still work for——'

'As from four o'clock this afternoon, *Leisure Days* doesn't exist. As from nine o'clock tomorrow morning you work for Magnum Enterprises; in other words, me.'

Stunned, Liza stared at him, her words of protest jamming painfully in her throat. She couldn't, she *wouldn't* work for him!

'This should take about an hour, Carl,' Robert Buchanan leaned forward to tell his chauffeur as they pulled up in the cobbled courtyard where a cluster of small architect-designed three-storey town houses were grouped.

'Do you want me to wait, sir?'

'No, Carl, take yourself off for some lunch, but be back by three—I've an appointment at three fifteen in Westminster.'

Somehow Liza's long legs carried her to her front door. She fumbled with the mortice lock, so sharply aware of him standing slightly behind her that her fingers felt stiff and clumsy. She heard the limousine reversing out of the courtyard, then her heartbeat racing inside her. This was ridiculous! Panic was rising unnecessarily. He'd offered her a job, wanted to talk about it over lunch in her home, and she understood why; nevertheless...

'A nice home you have,' he commented as she led him upstairs to the first-floor sitting-room. She took off her jacket and watched him warily as he stepped towards the window. 'A river view; very pleasant.'

'It's...it's even better from the bedrooms upstairs.'

She could have bitten her tongue out for that. Heat scorched her neck as lazily he turned to her and, with a sardonic smile creasing across his jawline, he said, 'Thanks for the offer but I came here to talk business, not to make love to you.'

'I...I didn't mean that!' she blurted self-consciously. Oh, he was quick, too sharp and suggestive by far.

'Didn't you?' He slid out of his suit jacket, flung it carelessly across her chintz Laura Ashley sofa. 'You wouldn't be the first woman to offer me her body within fifteen minutes of our relationship.'

Steeling herself, Liza decided there was only one way to deal with this man—bluntly!

'Takes that long, does it?' she iced. 'Don't bother to make yourself comfortable,' she blazed as he was about to lower himself on to the sofa. 'Pick up your jacket and march, Mr Robert Buchanan; we have nothing to say to each other, business or otherwise.'

He straightened up, a suggestion of a smile playing at the corners of his mouth. 'You can afford to be that choosy, can you?'

'What's that supposed to mean?'

'You're turning my business proposition down without hearing it?'

'All I've heard from you so far is filthy innuendoes about your carnal mating prowess!'

With a smirk he shook his left hand as if he'd been stung. 'Quite a bite you have,' he observed, 'and all I deserve. I'm sorry if I've upset you.'

'It would take more than the likes of you to upset me,' she replied haughtily. 'Like you, I get propositioned every day of my life. I can handle it; you obviously have a problem. I mean it: I'm not interested in anything you have to put to me. Shall I call you a taxi?'

She moved to the phone on the coffee-table as he lowered himself down to the sofa and settled himself back, the movement stretching his grey waistcoat across his broad chest. He was a powerfully built man and Liza was acutely aware of his physique. It disturbed her, and that was a stupid realisation.

'I'm not going anywhere, Liza,' he said smoothly. 'I've apologised once; I'm not in the habit of repeating myself. I want you, not your body, though the thought is very delectable. I'm not a fool; I don't mess with my employees. I want you to work for me and I don't take you for a fool either. To refuse me would be very unwise indeed.'

'That sounds remarkably like a threat to me.'

He looked up at her, jet eyes narrowed warningly. 'It is. You'd be wise to heed it.'

He lunged forward as defiantly Liza reached for the phone. His fingers wrapped around her wrist, not forcibly but firmly enough to convince her he meant business. She let go of the handset reluctantly.

'Good girl,' he patronised. 'Now, what about some lunch?'

Wrenching her wrist away from him, she glowered at him darkly. 'Last night's lasagne reheated in the microwave. It's all I have,' she clipped, knowing it was the only way to get rid of him. Feed him, listen to what he had to say and then, at three on the dot, slam the door after him. Thank you and goodbye, Robert Buchanan!

'The more I see of this house, the more I like it,' he said, following her into the small yet functional kitchen divided off from the sitting-room by a wide archway.

Liza slammed the microwave door shut on the lasagne and punched out five minutes on the digital timer. She refused to say a word. Her mouth had led her into enough trouble already.

'The mortgage on such a desirable residence in London must be quite a millstone for a single lady.'

She swung on him then, her flame hair flying wispily around her face. Impatiently she tucked it behind her ears. 'What's that supposed to mean? Are you implying I might supplement my income on the streets...?' Her voice cracked in protest at herself. He hadn't implied anything of the sort! 'I'm sorry,' she murmured, turning away to put on the kettle. 'I seem to be going slowly mad.'

'I disagree. You're heading for the funny farm very rapidly.'

Liza reluctantly smiled then, turning her wide green eyes to him leaning nonchalantly in the archway. 'You could be right,' she sighed, 'but it's not every day you lose your career.'

'Your career is just about to begin,' he told her blandly.

'You're going to make me an offer I can't refuse, are you?'

'I'd say you're not in a position to turn any offer away. Even a month out of work these days will play havoc with your bank account.'

'Very true,' she conceded, reaching for plates from the cupboard above her head. 'But you're not the only publisher in town. I've enough contacts in the business to get myself another position tomorrow.'

'Not when word gets round that *Leisure Days* folded because of mismanagement.'

'On the editorial side, not mine. I know my worth, Mr Buchanan.' She frowned suddenly. 'So why did you buy it?' she asked.

'It wasn't all bad. It has potential and it went for a song. I'll merge it with several others...'

'Clone it, don't you mean?' she retorted.

'Call it what you will, but in six months it will be the best monthly of its kind on the newsstands, here and across the continent,' he told her confidently.

'I'm not sure I want to work in that sort of stable. I like a small independent concern with a bit of character,' she told him resolutely.

The microwave pinged out its five-second warning as Robert Buchanan stated quietly, 'I'm not offering you the job.'

'Oh!' Her quizzical eyes settled on his. 'What exactly are you offering?'

'Overall advertising directorship. Thirty-five European magazines with offices in Amsterdam, Paris, Madrid...'

He reeled off several more capital cities, but Liza's head buzzed his words into a blur. The lasagne nearly hit the quarry-tiled kitchen floor.

With shaking fingers she lowered the dish to the work-surface.

'You've got to be joking!' she breathed incredulously.

'I don't make jokes about business. Do you want the job or not? I can name a hundred others who would rip their hearts out for such an offer.' He stepped forward and picked up the plates and cutlery Liza had laid out ready, and turned and took them into the dining section of the sitting-room.

Liza stood where she was, stupefied into senselessness by the thought of such a job. He couldn't be serious! This was some sort of weird hallucination. She plunged her index finger into the centre of the lasagne and winced at the pain of the burn. Yes, she was awake and this wasn't some crazy dream. She lifted the dish and carried it into the other room, went back into the kitchen, and made a pot of tea, hardly aware of what she was doing.

'This is delicious!' he enthused as he forked a mouthful. 'You're a good cook.'

'I'm not,' Liza told him, her voice a croaking whisper. 'There's an Italian take-away round the corner. 'I'm not a cook and I can't take your job...but thank you for the offer.'

The day-old lasagne was like layered cardboard in her mouth. She swallowed hard and poured two mugs of steaming tea.

'Your hand is shaking. What are you afraid of?'

She raised her eyes to his, tried to force a smile, but her pale coral lips twisted instead. She shook her head. 'I can't believe you've just offered me such a stupendous job; I mean ... it's ... it's too much ...'

'Oh, dear,' he sighed, laying down his fork. 'Don't say for the first time in my life I've made a wrong character judgement. You're not going all female on me, are you?'

'How do you mean?' her voice came back strongly.

'You don't feel you're capable of such a position?'

'No ... it's not that.' Oh, God, it was! She was good at her job and knew it, but this offer was out of this world. The thought of running such an empire terrified her and yet ... the challenge!

Robert Buchanan's hand reached out and touched hers across the glass-topped table. 'Liza, I wouldn't be making this offer if I didn't think you were right for it.'

'But you don't even know me!' Liza argued, drawing her hand away from his.

'I don't know half of my staff but I know *about* them, just as I know that your qualifications and your flair are right for the job. I've done my homework. You have communication talent, a shrewd head on your shoulders. You don't take any nonsense from anyone—you proved that with your attitude towards me.'

'I was rude to you,' she admitted, lowering her head.

'Not without cause. I made a tactless remark in front of people whose nerves were already on a knife-edge.'

She admired him for admitting to that, but it didn't change her opinion of him. He was ruthless. By what she had read about him, she knew he would dispense with the majority of the staff she had worked alongside. He wouldn't tolerate John Standish's ineptitude; he'd be on the next dole queue without a doubt. And what would become of her if she didn't jump when he commanded? He'd fire her without a qualm if she didn't prove her worth. But with a negative attitude like that she wouldn't go far in this world, she reasoned miserably.

'I'll quadruple your present salary.' He picked up his fork and proceeded to finish his lunch.

Liza watched him, cat-like. Money. Did he think it could be as easy as that?

'That's some carrot you're dangling.'

'Take it, before I offer it elsewhere,' he told her coldly.

He obviously thought she was playing hard to get. 'Why me?' she challenged. 'It's a heavyweight job, more suited to a man, I would have thought.'

'Most of my magazine staff are women. I like women. Don't you read the gossip columns?' He raised a sardonic black brow, questioning her.

'I read them, but I can hardly believe any man has the libido you are credited with.'

He smiled at that, a white smile that had melted many a foolish heart. Liza was unaffected by it, her iron resolve to stave off all men for life forcing her heart to granite hardness.

'I enjoy the publicity more than I do the women I'm supposed to have bedded. I'm a confirmed bachelor, you see,' he told her with a hint of a sparkle to his dark eyes.

'And I'm a confirmed spinster, so you and I just might get along.' She presented a sweet smile with that sweeping statement.

'One of the lesser reasons why I picked you for the job. You have the reputation for having a hard heart, Liza. No emotional involvement, not even an occasional bonding to while away a lonely night. You're good executive material. Graham Bond did a sterling heart-hardening job on you all right, didn't he?'

'You bastard!' Liza seethed through white lips. She would have got to her feet and slapped his supercilious face if she'd had the strength, but his harshness and cruelty had sapped every gram of fight out of her.

'I'm not, actually. I have a father, and he is alive and well.'

'I'm not doubting your parentage,' she parried. 'I was using the adjective in its degenerate form, and even then it's too good for you. How dare you muck-rake my past and fling it in my face so cruelly?'

'I wasn't aware I was doing any such thing. The point I'm trying to make is that you're not some silly flighty female who allows her head to be turned by the male species. You won't suddenly fly off and start breeding when the broody season comes.'

'You really are a mega-chauvinist rat, aren't you?' Gradually her strength was edging back.

'I've never been called that before but it certainly has a charming ring to it. Maybe you'd be better employed writing copy for some feminist rag, of which I own none, I might add.' He stood up and pulled his waistcoat down.

'In other words, you're retracting the offer I'm determined to refuse,' she shot back, getting to her feet and crashing the dirty plates together in a pile.

'On the contrary, the offer still stands. I still want you—on my staff, not in my bed, so quash any notions in that direction.'

'None exists,' she slammed back, 'and let me tell you, you have as much chance of getting into mine as a virulent flea.'

His grin was as wide as the ocean. 'Good. So long as we both know where we stand we should get on famously. I'll pick you up at eight-thirty in the morning, show you over your new office suite.'

'Don't bother. I won't be here. I'll be queuing up at the employment agency with all the other talent that you throw out on the slush pile!'

He picked up his jacket from the sofa, and turned to her with eyes glazed to coal-black hardness. 'Don't waste your energy, sweetheart; by the time I come off the phone tonight you'll be lucky to get a job licking stamps in any publishing mail-house.'

'Do what you will! But I'd rather stack shelves in a supermarket than work for you!' She teetered down the stairs after him, ready to slam the front door behind him in a last gesture of defiant independence. He took the wind from her sails by turning at the door and raising his hand to cup her chin.

'If it's any consolation I think you had a narrow escape with Bond. He wasn't man enough for you. And yet look what he's done to you. It would take a giant of a male ego to soften you into suppliance now and keep you there.'

To her shock and horror his mouth swooped down to hers, claimed her lips and held them with force and yet such deep sensuality that her head reeled. When he'd taken his fill he wiped the moisture from her swollen lips with his thumb.

'Don't get any ideas. That's my first and last show of weakness where you are concerned. I was just curious to know what you tasted like. If you did but know it, that glacial reserve of yours is totally transparent. You might have pulled up the drawbridge on your emotions but they are still there.' He tilted her chin once again. 'Soften up,

Liza; I wouldn't like to see my advertising director get hurt again.'

He turned and shut the door softly behind him, and for the first time in a very long time Liza Kay allowed a soft tear to trickle down her burning cheeks.

CHAPTER TWO

THE next morning when Liza awoke she knew she would take the job Robert Buchanan had offered. She'd be a fool not to, and yet she knew deep inside her that it wouldn't be easy.

Cupping her hands behind her head, she lay in the downy softness of her bed and wondered how Buchanan knew so much about her private life; but was it so surprising when he was practically omniscient?

Later Liza showered, and tied her hair back from her face with a green velvet ribbon that picked out the green in her Paisley-print shirt. She was careful with her make-up as usual. Endowed with a pale creamy skin that went with her flame hair, she was skilled at concealing the mass of freckles that bridged her nose and scattered her cheekbones. Her lashes were pale gold and she stroked them liberally with dark brown mascara to accentuate her startling green eyes. Graham had adored her eyes . . .

'To hell with Graham!' she muttered under her breath, and clipped huge gold orbs to her ears.

She smoothed the narrow tailored skirt of her favourite taupe wool suit, adjusted the shoulders of the jacket, and looked at herself in the mirror.

She looked every inch the successful executive, and yet inside she was trembling like a jelly.

'And damn Robert Buchanan!' she exhaled as she gathered up her Enny bag.

She was at the front door on the dot of eight-thirty, mildly disconcerted that Carl was the only occupant of the limousine that purred at the kerb-side. So what had she expected? The big white chief to pick her up in person?

'Where are we going, Carl?' she asked as she settled into the back seat.

'Knightsbridge, Miss Kay. The new block Mr Buchanan has just refurbished for Magnum.' He grinned in the rear-view mirror. 'Beauti-ful building, miss, and just a stone's throw from Harrods. Wonderful shopping in Knightsbridge...'

Liza was glad of his cheery conversation; it kept her mind off other things, namely Robert Buchanan. She still wasn't convinced it was a good idea to take this job, but if she thought of working for Magnum Enterprises, not the man himself, it helped...a bit.

The building was indeed magnificent. Glass and chrome and cool marble. She was greeted in Reception by a welcoming blonde receptionist, who took her up to the fifth floor of the block and handed her over to a David Cassals. He gripped her hand warmly.

'Pleased to meet you, Liza,' he grinned, running his eyes over her in undisguised approval. 'I'll show you to your office. Robert will join you later.'

Not wanting to sound gauche, she hid her delight at the pale grey carpeted suite of offices with its profusion of green plants and red and black hi-tech furnishings. It was a dream of a place to work in, with a view over a delightful square; though dreary now in the winter, it promised lush green pleasure for the summer. A world away from her cramped drab office in Soho.

'Coffee, tea or something stronger?' David grinned.

'Coffee would be nice,' she smiled back.

'My pleasure.'

He shut the door quietly behind him, and Liza was left alone in an insulated silence. She let out a long breath and lowered herself into a leather wing chair behind a matt black ash-wood desk. *Her* desk! It was almost too good to be true. Seconds later she jumped as the fax whirred. She leaned back and took the sheet of paper from the machine on the console behind her.

WELCOME

I'LL JOIN YOU FOR COFFEE

Robert

With a smile Liza balled the sheet of paper and tossed it into the waste-bin. Almost immediately the door opened and Robert Buchanan walked in with a tray of coffee and kicked shut the door behind him.

'So what changed your mind?' he asked, placing the tray down on the desk.

'I'm not stupid,' Liza commented and proceeded to pour the coffee. 'Stacking shelves won't pay the mortgage, will it?'

'No second thoughts?' He indicated the office suite with a nod of his dark head.

'Many, but my good sense overruled them. I'm ambitious, and this seems a good place to be ambitious in.' She handed him a coffee and pushed the sugar and cream towards him.

He perched on her desk and smiled at her. She glanced at his mouth, stemming the recall button on her mind: she didn't want to bring back that *frisson* that had shaken her when his mouth had closed over hers the previous day. He'd made it clear it wouldn't happen again. It was partly the reason she was here. She trusted him not to repeat it ever again.

'You were very sure I would come,' she said, and sipped her coffee.

'Yes, I was. So sure I had your stuff moved from the *Leisure Days* offices last night.'

'My stuff?'

He nodded to the desk drawer. Liza opened it. There was her folding mirror, a spare lipstick, a comb—nothing of great importance.

'You needn't have bothered.' She slammed the drawer shut, slightly annoyed at his presumption that she would take this position.

'I thought it would make you feel at home.'

She looked at him quickly. Such thoughtfulness. Somehow out of character. 'Thank you, but it wasn't necessary. I'm not a sentimentalist. One door closes and another opens, if you get my drift.'

'Ice drift, I'd say,' he said lazily. 'Now, what do you want to do about staffing? I've already got a team of seven telephone-sales people lined up for you, but is there anyone you want to bring over from Soho? David is the factotum around here, but you'll need a personal assistant.'

Julia! Liza's heart twisted guiltily. She hadn't given her assistant a thought. She hadn't returned to the office after lunch with Robert Buchanan. There hadn't seemed much point as the magazine was being folded that very afternoon.

'What happened to the staff? I didn't go back yesterday.'

'I've placed a lot of them elsewhere. There were casualties, of course.'

'John?'

'A hefty redundancy payment he didn't deserve.'

'So you have a heart after all.'

'The power of the Press,' he murmured, draining his coffee.

'Until I make my own judgement, that's all I have to go on,' she retaliated coolly. 'I'd like Julia to carry on working for me, if that's all right with you. She's been with me for three years and we work well together.'

'She has a weakness for the opposite sex, my sources tell me.'

Liza levelled cool green eyes at him. Was there nothing he didn't know? 'You have something in common with her, then.'

For only a second his jaw tensed angrily, then he gave a small smile. 'That's what I like about you. I could make and break you, but you still plough on, don't you? Beware, Liza; I can take so much and then I might be tempted to give you what you deserve.'

'And what might that be?'

'Push me far enough and you might find out. What you don't realise is that your puerile little insults could well turn out to be the turn-on of the decade for me. And maybe that's what you're working on. I might just take up the challenge you're throwing out to me.'

Colour flushed her neck and threatened her cheeks. 'I wasn't aware I was issuing one.' Trust him to twist everything she said his way.

'You're either remarkably astute or simply naïve. By your past record with men, I'd opt for the latter, but one thing I've learned in my thirty-seven years—never underestimate the wiles of women.'

She wasn't going to let that pass. 'It works both ways, you know. You tell me you don't mess with your employees, yet you couldn't keep your hands off me yesterday afternoon. You kissed me and then calmly told me it was a one-off. It's you who's remarkably astute or simply naïve,' she echoed stiffly. 'I'll opt for the former!'

'On the contrary, I think I'm rather making a fool of myself. Yesterday was a grave error on my part, but understandable. You're a very beautiful lady and the temptation to seduce you is great. I understand how you feel, too; women fall at my feet like ninepins.' There was a hint of humour in his eyes.

With a snort of disdain to cover her amusement at his inflated egotism, she told him flatly, 'There is no doubt that you are a very attractive animal. So is a Rottweiler, but I wouldn't give it house-room!'

To her surprise, he laughed. 'You really are the most amazing lady. So where do we go from here?'

She stood up and placed her empty coffee-cup on the tray. 'You have a choice: fire me or not.' She was playing with dynamite and knew it. But she had learnt a lot about him in this brief inter-change of insults. He was adept at winding her up, but she had the ability to do likewise to him. If he kept her on she'd put her heart and soul into her work; he knew that or he wouldn't have considered her in the first place. As for the per-sonal side of their relationship, it was going to be non-existent. She could handle him—of that she was sure. And he could handle himself!

'I wouldn't dream of firing you,' he told her, standing up. 'Not yet, that is.'

'Another threat?'

'More or less. And, as you so very rightly said, it works both ways. Neither of us can afford to get emotionally involved with each other. Let's both be warned off, shall we?'

He extended a hand to her in a gesture of goodwill, and Liza took it. He held on to her long enough to resurrect that *frisson* of awareness deep inside her. She was first to break the contact.

'What do you want me to do about Julia?'

'David can get in touch with her and she can start tomorrow.'

'Thank you,' Liza smiled.

'I'm not doing you a personal favour,' he assured her, dark brows drawn together seriously. 'But if you say she's good at her job I'll go along with it. Now, to work. I'll introduce you to your sales team. I'm afraid you're going to live in my pocket for the next few weeks. Working for Magnum is light years away from *Leisure Days*....' He took her arm and guided her out of the calm of her office into the mêlée of a frantic publishing house. And so her first day under Robert Buchanan's corporate umbrella began.

Three weeks later Liza stood by her sitting-room window, sipped her first coffee of the day, and realised that she was extremely happy. The job was panning out superbly. Robert had been right: she'd lived in his pocket, scarcely been out of his sight these past weeks. Her admiration for him had grown by the day. He knew his business all right, and his relationship with his staff was faultless. He had a knack of getting the best from everyone, and Magnum Enterprises rolled happily along on well-oiled wheels.

It started to rain again and Liza turned away from the window. As far as she could see there were no clouds on *her* horizon; even the pain of losing Graham had reduced to a small ache that only occasionally surfaced when she was particularly tired.

'I hate to ask, but could you bear a working weekend?' Robert suggested as soon as she arrived in her office that Thursday morning.

She looked at him in surprise. 'It's no problem for me, but what for? I thought everything was on schedule.'

'It is, but next week I want to introduce you to the European staff. We'll be going to Amsterdam for starters and then on to Paris and Madrid. It will mean at the very least a week out of here, and I want to make sure everything runs smoothly while we're away.'

Liza's heart raced at the thought. She was already liaising with the overseas advertising-sales offices and found it so stimulating she couldn't wait to get out there and meet these people in person.

'Sounds marvellous.' She grinned and picked up the unopened mail from her desk.

'Shouldn't Julia be dealing with that?' Robert observed quietly.

'She's at the dentist this morning.'

'Second time this week.'

Liza's eyes shot up from the envelope she was slitting. 'So?'

'Her teeth look perfectly all right to me.'

Liza tensed. 'What are you implying? That she's off out shopping somewhere?'

'Could be.' He shrugged his wide shoulders. 'But it's more than likely she's indulging herself in bed with Nigel Barnes from your sales team.'

Shocked, Liza let the letters fall to her desk. For some reason she didn't disbelieve him, knowing how fast Julia worked, but what really shook her was Robert's being the one to tell her.

'I think you must be mistaken...' she started to protest, colour flushing her cheeks. Robert had seen what she had failed to. Her first mistake.

'I'm not,' he assured her quietly.

Liza crossed the room and opened the door of her office. Nigel Barnes was conspicuous by his absence. All the sales team but him were at their consoles, busy on the phones.

She shut the door and went back to her desk. 'I'll deal with it,' she clipped tightly, and picked up the pile of letters.

'I'm sorry,' Robert said.

She glanced up at him. His face was ill at ease, a muscle pulsing at his throat. 'Sorry for pointing out what was staring me in the face, what I should have seen for myself?'

How stupid she had been. Julia's supposed dental appointments had coincided with Nigel's lateness. On Tuesday she had pulled him up on it, obviously to no effect. And he wasn't reaching his sales targets either. She had meant to deal with it sooner but pressure of other business had pushed it to the back of her mind.

'Nigel isn't reaching his targets...' Robert started to echo her thoughts.

'OK!' Liza suddenly stormed, and as quick as her temper flared it cooled, and she slumped down in her chair. 'I'm sorry; I'm just furious with myself for not seeing what was going on and dealing with it sooner.' She looked up at Robert standing so powerfully in front of the desk. He seemed to fill the room with his presence. 'I'll have a word with the pair of them.'

'A word isn't good enough, Liza; fire them before I do.' His voice was so deadly serious she felt a ping of dangerous apprehension down her spine.

Her lips tightened defiantly. 'Since when have you told me what to do with *my* staff?'

'Since when did you run Magnum?' he shot back.

Raking a tremulous hand through her hair, she calmed her stretched nerves. 'You gave me control over my advertising staff, Robert,' she reasoned coolly. 'Now you are trying to override me. Everyone deserves a second chance. You hired Nigel in the first place so you must have thought he had some worth, and I can't fault Julia—she's a damned good assistant. I don't like firing people without just cause.'

'And you think you haven't just cause?' He was angry now and Liza hadn't intended that. 'I don't care what my staff get up to outside of office hours, but when they do it in my time I see red——'

'You don't know anything for sure,' Liza argued.

'I know that I saw them all but having it off in the rest-room earlier this week——'

'Do you have to be so damned crude?' Liza interrupted furiously.

'Do you have to be so blind?' he raked back, his eyes glittering jets of fury. 'Because you're as cold as ice yourself you can't recognise sexual attraction in other people, even when it's flashed in front of your eyes in neon!'

Tears of pain stabbed the corners of her eyes. Shooting to her feet, she turned away from him, clutched her arms tightly around her shoulders and stared painfully out at the rain.

'That was unforgivable,' she croaked weakly, and then her whole body tensed alarmingly as he came up behind her and eased her clenched fingers from her shoulders. His own hands smoothed over the warm wool of her black sweater.

'I agree,' he murmured, so close she felt the warmth of his breath on the back of her neck. She suppressed the shudder his contact spun down her spine. 'It was unforgivable; nevertheless I apologise.'

Liza nodded her acceptance. 'If...if you knew what was going on between them,' she whispered, 'why didn't you dismiss them?'

'Because, as you rightly said, it's your place to deal with your own staff. I thought you would see it for yourself, but I realise now that I wasn't being wholly fair on you. A new job, a mountain of other responsibilities—I've expected too much of you too soon.'

She was about to protest that she was coping, but her words froze in her throat as the office door opened. Robert's hands flew from her shoulders as if he'd been stung, and Liza swung round so abruptly she nearly swayed into him.

'Don't forget the sales meeting at twelve,' Robert said curtly as he crossed to the door, where Julia stood blocking his way with a curious expression on her face. She moved aside to let him pass, closed the door after him and turned to Liza.

'I'm sorry my appointment took longer than expected,' she said brightly, easing out of her coat. Her tone implied she had seen nothing.

But she had; Liza knew that with a tightening of her stomach muscles. Julia couldn't have failed to see Robert Buchanan's hands on his advertising director's shoulders. Robert was almost all things, but an actor he wasn't. The curtness of his voice hadn't shadowed his guilt at all.

With a deep sigh Liza turned back to the mail; now wasn't the time to dress Julia down for her conduct with Nigel. Julia could easily misinterpret what she had seen. The way her mind worked she wouldn't see it the way it had been, even if Liza explained that Robert had been simply offering her an apology for his rudeness. And worse, if she did try to talk her way out of it, she would have to explain why she and Robert had argued in the first place.

Liza silently cursed her assistant's lack of discretion. She had enough to cope with without this!

She did tackle Nigel later, though; called him into her office when Julia wasn't around.

'I'm sorry to have to tell you this, Nigel, but the other sales staff are way ahead of you. You've only managed to sell two half-pages this week and that's not good enough.'

He blushed deeply, flicked his fair hair back from his forehead. 'Yes, well, I haven't settled yet. The place I worked before wasn't so fast——'

'I'm not concerned with your past,' she interrupted softly. She understood why Julia was attracted to him. He was good-looking in the young Robert Redford mould and had a soft, persuasive voice that was ideally suited to telephone sales. She'd looked up his CV before tackling him and he had glowing references from his last job; nevertheless...

'I regret bringing this up, but is your relationship with Julia affecting your work?'

He smiled without looking at her, which slightly annoyed Liza. 'You don't miss much, do you?'

If only he knew, Liza thought dismally, that someone else had had to spell it out to her.

'I don't want to pry into your private life, but if it overlaps into your working hours and loses money for the company I'll have to let you go; it's as simple as that.' She hoped she didn't sound too brutal, but Robert had made himself quite clear on how he felt and she certainly wasn't going to jeopardise her position for Nigel's sake.

'So you're telling me to stop seeing Julia, or else?' His blue eyes widened appealingly. Liza held them with the cool green of hers. He might have swept Julia off her feet with that look, but she was immune to tricks like that.

'I said nothing of the sort. I'm not concerned with your love-life but your sales target: you're not hitting it.' She took a sheet of paper from a file on her desk. 'Look, here's a list of advertisers that might help you. I've dealt with them in the past, though you'll have to do some hard selling—they aren't easy. See what you can do. I'll give you another week, and be sensible, Nigel. You've been late twice this week and you're not thinking wisely. This is a top organisation and you have a bright future with us if you knuckle down. Believe me, I don't want to lose you but I will if I must.'

She left it at that, hoped it would be enough, prayed it wouldn't come back on her. It did. Immediately after lunch.

'Nigel tells me you're not happy about our relationship,' Julia snapped at Liza as she swept back into the office. 'That's rich, coming from you.'

Liza aborted the phone call she was about to make, sat back, and gazed at her assistant. 'Would you like to enlarge on that?'

'It's all right for you to carry on with the boss——'

'I'm doing nothing of the sort!' Liza responded quickly, trying to keep her cool.

'So what I saw this morning was a figment of my imagination? You weren't in each other's arms?' She raised her eyebrows, daring Liza to deny it.

For the first time Liza doubted her judgement in bringing Julia to Magnum. She sensed she was going to give her trouble, take advantage of their past easy relationship.

She explained as best she could, without giving too much of her personal life away, how Robert Buchanan had come to have his hands on her. 'So in a way it was all your fault,' Liza finished with a touch of humour to lighten the atmosphere.

To her relief Julia gave her a wide grin and her hazel eyes twinkled mischievously. 'Just give me a nod and a wink if you need any more help in that direction.'

Liza held her hands up in mock defence. 'Forget it. I've no interest in our esteemed employer other than work-wise, thank you.'

'Says you,' laughed Julia, swinging into her own office off Liza's. She turned at the door. 'Thanks for sticking up for us, Liza. I *was* at the dentist, by the way. I've a crown to prove it. I can't account for Nigel's lateness, but I am seeing him and I promise not to let our affair show in office hours. I like working here and I don't want to lose my job.'

As Liza picked up the phone she wondered why she should feel so oddly apprehensive. It was the 'says you' comment from Julia that had unsettled her. She tapped out a code on the phone. She definitely hadn't got a personal interest in Robert Buchanan, but how easily that sort of gossip could rear its ugly head!

'You look worn out,' Robert told her, striding into her office after everyone had left at the end of the day.

'I feel it.' She stretched wearily like a lazy cat, not at all offended by his comment on her appearance. 'It's the take-away again tonight; I haven't the energy to boil an egg.'

'Is that a hint for me to offer dinner?' He smiled and plunged his hands into his trouser pockets.

'No way,' she laughed, crossing the room to pick up her jacket. 'You've caused enough trouble today.'

He helped her into her jacket and she let him. 'What's that supposed to mean?' he said.

'Nothing,' she told him lightly. No point in repeating gossip; it would only cause trouble for Julia, and things had gone smoothly all afternoon. 'Take a look at this.' She picked up a sheet of paper from her desk, diverting his attention back to work. 'I had a word with Nigel earlier on and it worked wonders. He's got a double-page spread from Citroën, to be repeated in five of our mags.'

Robert raised an impressed brow as he glanced at the paper. 'Not confirmed, though,' he murmured.

Liza laughed. 'Don't be such a pessimist. I've dealt with them before. They won't pull out.'

'So it was your idea he approached them?'

'Partly. I had a word with him about not reaching his targets and gave him a list of people I'd dealt with in the past, to sort of encourage him on. It worked.' She picked up her handbag. She was pleased Nigel had acted on it, almost immediately too, and was pleased with herself for not taking Robert's advice to throw him out.

'You might as well have done the job yourself. What's the point of keeping a dog and barking yourself?'

She was surprised at the sudden frown creasing his brow. To her astonishment she realised that Mr all-powerful Buchanan was looking pretty whacked-out himself. So he was human after all.

'I didn't do the job myself; I offered some guidance, that's all. That's what I'm here for, Robert,' she told him levelly. 'It's my job to oversee the advertising-sales operation.' She wasn't getting through to him. He still looked doubtful. 'I gave him a verbal warning about Julia too,' she added. 'I'm sure we won't have any more trouble from either of them again. By the way, she *was* at the dentist.'

Robert swept his fingers through his jet hair. 'I would rather have got rid of them. Can't say I've taken to either of them.'

'You don't have to like all your staff, do you?'

Robert held the door open for her and they headed for the lifts.

'I'd like to think it was possible,' he murmured. 'But I have an odd feeling about them.'

'I think you're over-reacting,' she told him, but said nothing about her own doubts, partly because she couldn't quite decipher them herself. Just an unease that was there, but wasn't in a way. Fatigue shrugged away the thoughts.

'If you won't join me for dinner, at least let Carl drop you off home. I'm on my way to Chelsea so it's no problem.'

Liza was grateful for the offer and accepted it graciously. There was little conversation in the back of the limousine, no need for idle chat. Three weeks together and they had slid into an easy relationship. Liza mused on those thoughts as the car moved sluggishly through rush-hour traffic. She smiled too—Robert had dozed off, and it was nice to think that he wouldn't have dreamt of doing such a thing in front of any of his other staff. Apart from that small altercation today they were getting on extremely well.

Carl came off the Kings Road and minutes later they pulled up outside a bijou town house in a small square.

'Mr Buchanan, sir. We're here.'

Robert stirred, adjusted his navy suit jacket and got out. 'Thanks Carl; you're off for the night, aren't you? Just drop Miss Kay off and that will be all. Goodnight, Liza.'

He turned and sprinted up the front steps of the house, and the door opened wide, spilling warm light out on to the street. A woman greeted Robert Buchanan, a woman in silhouette. She turned, and light flooded her face and hair. She was stunning, and obviously so delighted to see Robert that Liza felt like a voyeur as she watched them embrace each other and then, locked together, turn into the seclusion of the house.

'That's Lady Victoria Desprite,' Carl volunteered as he pulled away from the kerb. 'Quite something, isn't she?'

Liza felt as if her body had turned to granite, and yet her brain was functioning, buzzing wildly, uncontrollably. She couldn't answer Carl, couldn't comment on the beautiful woman who had such an impact on her heart.

'Actually, miss, don't think I'm getting fresh or anything, but you're not dissimilar, both got that lovely red hair...'

Though Battersea was but a stone's throw from Chelsea, the drive seemed to take an eternity. Liza wanted the security of her home, needed it badly. She was afraid, terribly afraid of this strange feeling inside her. What was it? Hurt? Jealousy? Perhaps disappointment that he hadn't *insisted* on taking her out to dinner? It had been a throw-away invitation, not meant to be taken seriously; after all, that lovely redhead had been expecting him. So what would have happened if she had said 'Yes, dinner sounds lovely; thank you for asking me—let's go!' Would he have cancelled Lady Victoria?

'God, I'm jealous!' she cried after slamming her front door after her and slumping back against it breathlessly. 'I can't be! It's bloody impossible!'

Yes, it was impossible, she decided as she soaked in the bath later. Impossible! She was tired, irritable with work today. That business with Nigel and Julia had rattled her. She bit her lip forcibly. She didn't, she wouldn't allow her emotions to go one step further. She liked Robert Buchanan, liked working for him. He had a reputation with women and she wasn't about to appear on his notch-belt of conquests! Suddenly she smiled to herself. Who was she kidding? He wasn't in the least bit interested in her! Three weeks virtually living in his pocket and not once had he stepped out of line. So what was she worried about? Closing her eyes and sliding down under the foam, she murmured, 'Nothing, nothing at all.'

CHAPTER THREE

IT SEEMED a cruel coincidence that a gossip columnist ran Robert Buchanan's relationship with the lovely Lady Victoria as his leader for the next day in Julia's newspaper.

Julia couldn't wait to tell Liza. She tossed the paper down on Liza's desk with a whoop.

'Brilliant, isn't he?' she cried. 'Don't you just love all this? Our boss, swanning around with society's most eligible lady. Look, there's a picture of them together at Krystals night-club last week. The papers reckon it's the real thing for them both this time. They've both got a hefty track record and...'

Liza pushed the paper aside and studied a sheet of sales figures and tried not to hear any more. Gossip. The newspapers thrived on it. Part of her felt sorry for Robert—hadn't he told her he was a confirmed bachelor? The rest of her decided it served him right for allowing the Press to hound him so. After all, he'd admitted he enjoyed his publicity. Damn! What did she care anyway?

She changed the subject, and subtly turned Julia's attention to her work. Julia soon forgot Robert Buchanan's love-life, and ploughed through a pile of letters Liza dictated to her. Liza, to her profound irritation, found she wasn't so easily distracted. Throughout the morning she kept bringing back to mind the embrace she had witnessed on the doorstep of that smart house in Chelsea. Fortunately, pressure of work in the afternoon forced all personal thoughts from her head.

'Don't worry about those,' Liza told Julia at five as she was about to scoop up a pile of artwork one of the advertisers had just courier-delivered for approval. 'I'll deal with them. I'm working over the weekend.'

Julia's face brightened. 'Overtime? Do you need me? I could do with some extra in my wage packet.'

Liza shook her head. 'No, Julia, but thanks for the offer. Robert will be here. We're going to Amsterdam next week and we have to tie things up before we go.'

She might have known Julia would take it all the wrong way.

'Cooped up here with the delicious Buchanan all weekend and zooming off to Amsterdam, eh? I wonder what Lady V will have to say about that?'

Liza's green eyes narrowed warningly. 'Enough of that—you're beginning to sound like those sensation-seeking dailies you pore over every morning.' She smiled suddenly. 'If you're offering your services for the weekend does that mean you and Nigel are cooling off?'

'Not likely,' Julia beamed, 'but this time I'm putting work before pleasure. Nigel and I are planning a spring break together—Marrakech or somewhere equally romantic. I could do with some extra cash.'

'In all the time I've known you,' Liza laughed, 'I've never known you to put your finances before a man, but I suppose the incentive this time is different.'

'It is; *this time* I'm really in love,' Julia twinkled.

The phone rang and Julia answered it. 'It's your mother,' Julia mouthed as Liza took the receiver from her. Julia went back to her office to tidy up before leaving.

It had completely slipped Liza's mind to phone her parents to say she wouldn't be over Sunday afternoon as usual. Her parents were sticklers for routine.

'Yvonne's pregnant, dear. I rang to ask if you'd like to come down to Wales with us to celebrate. You've never been, and your father and I...'

Her parents had never known of the intensity of her relationship with Graham. They had known of course that they were seeing each other and had accepted the switch of affections to their younger daughter without a qualm. Yvonne had known, of course. Hadn't she thrown herself at Graham when she'd realised just how serious Liza was? She'd done that since birth, wanted anything and everything that belonged to her sister. And now she was having Graham's child...

Robert stepped into Liza's office as she was explaining to her mother that she would be working over the weekend. When she finally put the receiver down her face was burning as if she had a fever.

'Family problems?' he quizzed.

'No... no, my mother calling. I'd made arrangements to see my parents Sunday, the usual duty call. I told her I was working.'

'Under normal circumstances I'd say go ahead and don't disappoint her, but I really do need you this weekend,' he said with a smile.

'It isn't a problem,' she assured him, trying to quell the terrible ache inside her that her mother's news had dealt.

'By the flush on your face, I'd say it was,' he persisted.

'With my colouring I flush at the slightest provocation,' she told him pointedly. 'Surely that hasn't passed your notice?' With a glance at her watch she started to tidy her desk.

'Well, I'm about to send you scarlet. Pack a weekend bag. We're working from my home in the country this weekend. I'll pick you up tonight at seven.' He strode out of her office before she could protest.

Would she have protested? she asked herself as later she threw a few essentials into an overnight bag. It wasn't out of order to work from his home. Hardly seemed worth heating the Magnum offices just for the two of them. She shivered as she zipped up the bag. The weather was appalling. Surely it couldn't rain much more?

At least if she was wrapped up in work all weekend she couldn't dwell on the thought of Graham and Yvonne and the baby. That baby was going to create a problem. She was going to be an auntie and she couldn't make many more excuses not to pay them a visit. She had avoided it so far, hadn't been able to bear witnessing their happiness, but one day...

'What's wrong?' Robert asked as they headed out of town. 'You seem very preoccupied with your thoughts. I hope you're not too disappointed at not visiting your parents this weekend.'

She turned to him then, realised she had been in a bit of a daze since he had picked her up. She hadn't even given much thought to the fact that Robert was driving his own car, a comfy Jaguar saloon, and was dressed as she had never seen him before—casually.

His dark grey cords emphasised the strength of his long legs, and the red of his polo-necked sweater seemed to draw out his darkness, yet softened the colour of his eyes and added a warmth to his jet hair. He certainly was an attractive man, probably more handsome and charismatic than Graham, and if she weren't still so hopelessly in love with her brother-in-law she might allow herself a thrill of excitement at the prospect of spending the weekend with him.

Liza forced a smile. 'I was just wondering about the weather. This rain doesn't seem to be letting up.'

Robert turned and gave her a doubtful look. 'I don't think for a minute you were thinking any such thing, but I must admit it's going on a bit.' He flicked a dial on the dashboard and warm air cleared the windscreen. 'It's why we're going down to my country house to work. I've a flat in town but I haven't been to the house for a few weeks. I've a lake in the grounds and my housekeeper informs me the level is getting dangerously high. I've some precious shrubs and trees I don't want to see drowned.'

Her smile wasn't forced this time. 'You don't strike me as being a gardening expert.'

'Hybrid fuchsias are my passion. I've a conservatory massed with them. Do you like fuchsias?'

Gradually Liza started to relax. They talked for a while about plants and flowers, though Liza wasn't knowledgeable enough to offer much herself. Robert did most of the talking and held her attention with his enthusiasm.

'That's better,' he smiled as they turned on to the motorway. 'I seemed to have cheered you up.'

'Yes, you have,' she admitted, and to her astonishment admitted more. 'My mother wanted me to go to see my sister and Graham this weekend. Yvonne is expecting a baby.'

Robert frowned. 'It still bothers you, does it?'

She regretted opening up to him, but it was done now and perhaps a bit of therapy might help.

'I was in love with him,' she told him softly, 'thought he loved me. My sister took him away from me. That's hard to live with as well.'

'I have no wish to hurt you further, but surely you're sensible enough to realise that his feelings for you obviously weren't as deep as yours? If he truly cared for you your sister couldn't have enticed him away.'

'What the hell would you know about people's feelings?' she clipped, fidgeting uncomfortably in her jeans. She didn't need him of all people to tell her what she didn't want to hear.

'True, I've never been in love—managed to avoid it like the plague all my life—but I'm sure if I did succumb I wouldn't allow it to blind me.'

Liza said miserably, 'I'm not blind. Don't you think I reasoned all that out for myself? It doesn't alter the fact that my sister made a play for him. If she hadn't Graham and I would have been married now.'

'And is that what you wanted, still want?' he challenged.

'I . . . yes, I wanted to marry him. I loved him.'

'Loved him, past tense. Don't you mean you love him—even after the blow he dealt you you still live in the hope that he might come back to you?' He shook his head. 'I thought you were made of sterner stuff.'

'I am!' she insisted, staring out at rain and more rain. She bit her lip. 'I wouldn't have him back if he crawled on his knees.'

'I should hope not. You might be a fool where he's concerned but I'm sure you're not a marriage-breaker, especially now there is a baby on the way.'

The finality of those home truths bit into the core of her being. Maybe Robert was right and all this time she had been nurturing the thought that Graham might realise what he had given up and want her back. Now it was an impossibility. She knew Graham well enough to know he wouldn't welsh on his duties. Poor Graham. Yvonne had certainly got all she wanted with scant regard for his needs. Babies and fatherhood had never entered her relationship with him. She wondered how his writing would go from here. Screaming children would hardly be conducive to his creativity.

'How did you know about my affair with him?' Liza asked after a while. They'd turned off the motorway now and were heading for Berkshire.

'A good friend of mine is his agent. When Bond's book narrowly missed the Booker Prize last year he got a lot of publicity, and he came up in conversation at a dinner party one night. We were talking about writers and writing, and Paul had been impressed by the dramatic change in Bond's style after his marriage.'

'So how did I come into this?' Liza asked.

Robert let out a ragged sigh. 'You really want to know?'

'Of course!' And she meant it. Somehow this purging was helping, in a masochistic sort of way.

'Bond couldn't write with you; told Paul that you stifled him. Yvonne was different, didn't expect him to rush around art exhibitions and clutter his mind with things he didn't want to do.'

'In other words, I was the kiss of death to his creativity,' Liza frosted back. Graham had tried to explain but she had been so numbed with shock that she hadn't taken it in.

'It's an interesting theory, don't you think?'

'Interesting maybe, but not true. Graham would have made it with me, it was just a question of adjustment. Yvonne caught him at a vulnerable time. He'd just had another rejection...' Oh, God, who was she trying to fool?

'Go on,' Robert urged quietly. 'You're getting it all out of your system.'

'That's the point of this conversation, is it?'

'Partly. I doubt if you've opened yourself up about it before.'

'Why should you be so interested?' she retorted.

'Because I don't like to see you going to waste. I told you before, you're well rid of him. The sooner you realise that, the better.'

'The better for whom?'

'You and the next man who breaks your reserve and makes love to you.'

'I don't intend to repeat my mistakes,' she retorted bitterly. 'Once bitten, twice shy, et cetera, et cetera.'

'Harsh vows for a woman of your beauty to take. Don't tell me you don't ache for a man at times.'

She was grateful for the blackness of the country lane they were sloshing down. It concealed the flame of her cheeks, the give-away pain in her eyes.

'I'm human,' she admitted in a whisper. 'When the time comes I might consider giving myself to another man—my body, not my heart,' she added poignantly.

'Jeezus,' he breathed irritably. 'Heaven forbid that I should be that man. You sound as if you'll be bestowing the gift of the century. Don't prize your body to that degree, Liza.'

'I didn't mean it to sound like that,' she murmured. 'I don't want another involvement, that's all. I don't want to be hurt again.'

He said nothing more. They drove on in silence, the wind and rain lashing the windscreen. Once or twice Liza glanced at him, frowned at the grim set of his features. He was obviously worried about the lake flooding his precious trees. She wished they had continued that line of conversation instead of analysing her. She wondered what powered him through life. Had someone hurt him in the past to give him this cavalier attitude with women? Was Lady Victoria about to break his resolve of confirmed bachelorhood? Would a man ever break her own vows of non-involvement?

She eased back in her seat and closed her eyes. Strange, but she could imagine Robert Buchanan to be the sort of man to break down her reserves. She admired him greatly. He was strong and powerful, ran an enviable empire, was respected. He had charm and wit and almost everything a woman could wish for. Yes, he was the *sort* of man who might turn her on, but not *the* one. Yesterday, she thought, she had experienced jealousy seeing Robert with that beautiful woman. It had been jealousy, though not because of them but their situation. She envied people free to love each other. Maybe now was the time for her to start to ease up on her own emotions.

'Why the sudden smile?' Robert spoke softly and Liza's heart jerked. Sometimes his faint accent showed through, like now. It was very attractive.

Liza opened her eyes. 'I was just doing a bit of soul-searching.' Almost true. For a moment she had allowed her imagination to run amok, imagined she was his lover and they were spending this weekend doing everything else but work. It had been an amusing thought. The ice was thawing, if she could fantasise that way.

Robert didn't press her. The road ahead was occupying him fully.

'I don't like the look of this,' he said in a gravelly voice. 'The road has started to flood. There's a reservoir around here somewhere; it must have overflowed. I've never seen conditions like this before.'

'Have we much further to go?' Liza asked, but Robert didn't answer. They hit a sheet of water, and Liza's seatbelt jerked her back into her seat.

'Are you all right?'

'Fine.'

Minutes later they shushed into a wide driveway, but it was so dark and wet Liza could barely see the house ahead.

'Don't suppose you thought to bring an umbrella?' he asked. She shook her head. 'We'll have to make a run for it.'

They did, but got soaked in the process. Robert opened up the house, flicked on lights and dashed back to the car for Liza's bag and a stack of paperwork he'd haphazardly thrown on to the back seat. Liza scarcely had time to take in her surroundings before Robert crashed back into the house, slamming the front door behind him and spilling files to the floor.

He was soaked through to the skin, his hair plastered to his head.

'You'd better get out of those clothes before you catch pneumonia,' she told him, shaking a spray of water from her own mass of flyaway hair. She scooped it back from her rain-speckled face, her heart pulling wildly at the expression in his eyes. For a split second she smelled danger, was so conciously aware of it that it shocked her. It wasn't a fear brought on by the wind and rain raging outside, but of the look in his eyes.

His hand came up, and she flinched as he smoothed the rain from the bridge of her nose. 'Freckles,' he murmured. 'I've never noticed them before. You look about twelve years old.'

Too quickly she darted away from him and crouched on the floor to gather up the papers. He hauled her to her feet, held her away from him to look her in the face.

'What are you afraid of?' His eyes darted across hers, trying to measure the green brightness.

'I'm...I'm not afraid,' she stammered untruthfully. A shudder ran through her, one he registered. She covered it with, 'I'm just cold and wet.'

He let her go, she imagined it was reluctantly, then dismissed the idea with a fevered toss of her senses.

'We'd both better get changed, then a stiff drink might be a good idea.' He picked up her bag. 'Follow me; I'll show you to your room.'

Liza did as he bid, and trotted after him to the first floor.

The double-fronted country house was deliciously warm, and her feet sank into inches of wall-to-wall luxury. Her fleeting glance at the furnishings noted usable antiques and Regency drapes at the windows. Her room was lovely, soft pinks and watery green, and now, fully recovered from the shock of his touching her nose so intimately, she enthused her delight.

'It's a gorgeous room.' She crossed to the window, and cupped her hands around her face to shut off the light so she could see out better. It was so black outside that it didn't help, but she caught a glimpse of silvery-grey water. 'Is that the lake? It's practically on the doorstep.'

Suddenly Robert was at her side, swinging up the window and receiving a shower of rain full in the face. Unheeded, he leaned out and peered into the darkness.

'Doesn't look good,' he grated, closing the window. He turned to Liza. 'Get out of those wet jeans and take a shower then we'll have a drink and eat; you must be starving—I am.' He left her to unpack, and Liza let out a ragged breath as he shut the door behind him. He'd unnerved her downstairs—her own fault for reacting so unnecessarily tightly to his touch and the look in his eyes. He hadn't meant anything by it.

The bathroom off the bedroom was luxury itself. She opted for a soak rather than a shower. He was obviously a good host and the array of bath oils and fragrant toiletries held her rapt for a while.

'Oscar de la Renta tonight,' she murmured, and liberally squirted the swirling bath water with the essence.

She lingered too long in the bath. Stepped out with too healthy a glow on her face. She tried to play it down by slipping into a dark green velvety jogging suit: green was supposed to be good for disguising high colour, she'd heard. It wasn't as effective as she'd hoped. Oh, well, he'd seen her freckles; no good fighting them any more.

She ran barefoot down the stairs, heard movement coming from the left and followed it. Robert was in the cosy countrified kitchen, stirring a casserole before putting it back into the Aga.

'Smells delicious. Is cooking another of your talents?' she asked lightly.

He turned, not having heard her approach, and frowned darkly, his eyes sweeping over her.

Liza sensed an atmosphere, was bewildered by it.

'My housekeeper does my cooking. Stocks the fridge and freezer for me,' he said shortly. He turned his attention to a bottle of red wine on the kitchen table. He poured two glasses before asking if she wanted something stronger. Seeing as he'd already poured the wine, she took that as presuming if it was all right for him it was OK with her.

'The wine is fine,' she returned, for the first time noticing the pile of paperwork stacked on the table.

'As we have so much to plough through I hope you don't mind a working dinner.' His tone was clipped and formal, just as he was in the office most times when dealing with business. It mildly surprised Liza. She hadn't expected a relaxing weekend, but she had expected to unwind a little before getting down to it.

She sat at the table, pulled the pile of projects towards her and started to leaf through them. 'That's what we're here for, isn't it?' she said in a low voice, concentrating hard on the figures that swam before her. She was already tired, she realised; it hadn't been an easy week and, what with the drive down here as well...

'Is it?' he said softly, stepping towards her and pulling out a wheelback chair from the dark oak table. He sat down and stretched his long legs under the table. He had changed into a black tracksuit for relaxation, but relaxing he wasn't. His face looked drawn.

Liza ignored the question, and fought to keep her eyes on the work in front of her.

'Maybe I don't know myself as well as I thought. Maybe I want to make love to you all weekend instead of working,' he said quietly.

Her head jerked up at that. Her eyes opened wide. Was he testing her, or was it his sense of humour at work?

'That sounded like a reluctant admission,' she forced to her lips, surprised that her palms felt so hot and sticky.

'It wasn't an admission; more reluctant speculation.'

'Do you expect me to respond to it?' She tried to sound cool and offhand but it was an effort. She was a fool to have agreed to come to his home. His experience of life far outweighed hers. He was pushing her into realms she was incapable of handling, and yet she'd held her own with him before; no reason why she couldn't handle this.

She folded her arms across her chest and leaned back in her chair. 'You know it would be foolish.'

'Very,' he agreed with a hint of a smile, 'but sometimes in one's life one is allowed to lapse.'

'This isn't one of those times, Robert.'

'You push me to the limits, though. Are you aware of that?'

'No, I'm naïve, don't forget. You said so yourself.'

'I think you know exactly what you're about,' he suggested, his smile twisting to a smirk. 'I don't remember your uttering a word of protest at the suggestion of working from my home this weekend.'

Frissons of anger pulsed through her. Why, oh, why hadn't she seen this coming?

'I trusted you,' she told him honestly. She had. Not for a minute had she thought she would be fighting for her honour in so short a time.

'Trusted a man with my supposed reputation?' he drawled sarcastically.

'It's not supposed,' she argued. 'You *have* a reputation—the papers scream it out. Only this morning——'

'Only this morning they have me married off to Vicky. Do you believe all that trash reporting?'

'I saw it with my own eyes,' she retorted fiercely. 'You were with her last night!' She bit her lower lip at her outburst.

Robert was quick to take up on it. 'And what went through your mind?'

'Not a lot. Sorry to be a disappointment but I didn't lie awake all night mulling it over.'

'Well, I did. I wanted to take you out to dinner but you slid out of it expertly. That bothered me a great deal because I would rather have spent the time with you instead of an empty-headed socialite.'

Stunned, Liza stared at him idiotically.

'That surprises you, does it? It shocked the living daylights out of me, I can tell you.' He moved back to the Aga and brought the steaming casserole to the table.

She didn't understand him. Why was he admitting his attraction to her when he had already said he didn't want an involvement with her? She supposed that as they were out of the normal working environment he thought he could get away with talking that way.

Liza watched him dish up two enormous platefuls, doubting she'd be able to get a mouthful down. If he carried on flirting with her she was certain she wouldn't!

He didn't, and her stomach was grateful. 'Home cooking,' she murmured. 'It's wonderful.' She forced herself to sound casual in the hope it wouldn't give him any more ideas.

Halfway through the meal he poured more wine, pulled the pile of paperwork towards him and then work began in earnest. Soon they were both engrossed, eating and talking and finishing the wine.

'I'll make the coffee,' Liza offered after a while. She needed it to keep her eyes open. The warmth of the kitchen, the satisfying meal and the headiness of the wine had sapped her strength.

Robert murmured his thanks, his head bent over paperwork. She found all she needed, and as she waited for the water to boil she stretched her aching limbs and leaned back against the Aga towel-rail to look at him. What an unusual man and what a strange situation this was, she mused. A powerful publishing magnate conducting his business over a kitchen table littered with domestic paraphernalia—dirty dishes, greasy wine glasses. She went to the table to clear them. His hand snaked out to stop her.

'Leave it; I don't expect you to clear up. I have staff coming in in the morning.'

'At least let me pile the dishes in the sink,' she said, drawing her hand away from his.

He stretched wearily. 'Don't bother. I'm bushed now, and you must be exhausted as well.' He stood up slowly. 'We'll take our coffee into the sitting-room and relax for a while.'

She shrugged. 'That's not necessary. It's warm and relaxing in here. No point in messing up another room.'

With a smile he sank back into the chair. 'How simple and easy life with you would be,' he said.

Liza poured the coffee and brought it to the table, pushing aside the dirty dishes to make room. 'Because I want to drink my coffee in here? It's a lovely kitchen. I've always thought that houses should be designed around kitchens. Have you noticed, at parties, everyone congregates around the kitchen sink?' Was she going over the top, striving for normality too hard?

'Not at the sort of parties I attend,' he mused.

She'd asked for that. Silly of her to imagine the circle he prowled in would entertain in a lowly kitchen. Lady Victoria probably didn't even know where hers was!

She drank her coffee in the hope it would rouse her, but finally had to succumb to tiredness.

'I'll go up if you don't mind. I'm nearly falling asleep.' She stood up, somewhat shakily. 'What time do you want to start in the morning?'

'When you're ready,' he told her. 'I won't slave-drive you this weekend.'

'Goodnight, then.'

'Liza.'

She stopped at the door and turned to him. He was still sitting at the table, his back to her.

'Come here,' he commanded softly; nevertheless a command.

She went to him, stood by his chair. He seemed to take forever raising his head to look at her. Slowly he lifted his hand, linked it gently round her neck and pulled her down towards him. His mouth was soft and warm on hers, a kiss that roused her senses and flooded her with emotions that confused her. She didn't pull away but allowed herself a second for blissful heat to course through her body. His mouth stayed passive against hers, demanding nothing more but the pleasurable silkiness of her lips.

She drew away from him, and he turned his face away from her so she could read nothing in his eyes.

'Goodnight, Liza,' he murmured, reaching out for the empty wine bottle and draining the dregs into his glass.

She fled without a word, flew up to her room as if hell-fire were scorching her heels. He shouldn't have done that, her mind screamed, her nerves inflamed with anger. He shouldn't tease me this way, it's unfair, so very unfair.

CHAPTER FOUR

LIZA woke up in the middle of the night with a raging thirst. Groping for the bedside light, she clicked it on. Nothing. She lay still for a while, trying to rouse herself fully before attempting to stagger around in the dark. There was a faint roaring sound. It seemed to be in the room, but when she concentrated hard she realised it was coming from outside. More rain?

The central heating was off and Liza wrapped the warm duvet round her, willing her thirst away. It wouldn't go. Reluctantly she hauled herself out of bed, pulling her baggy cotton nightgown down over her thighs. She groped her way to where she thought the bathroom was and walked into the wall, bumping her head. It brought her fully awake and she cursed softly under her breath.

Finding the bathroom, she flicked the light-switch. Nothing again. A power-cut, obviously. She felt for the glass she knew was by the sink and filled it with water from the tap. One mouthful and she spat it out. It was bitter and left a metallic taste in her mouth that accentuated her thirst. She recalled there was bottled water downstairs, in the cupboard where she'd found the coffee. She shivered at the prospect of lurching around in the cold and darkness.

Her eyes became accustomed to the darkness and, clutching the banister, she went downstairs. Somehow she missed her footing and, stumbling down the last few, landed with a scream of terror in icy cold water.

'Robert! Oh, God, Robert!'

Her head swam sickeningly and she struggled to her feet, grasping wildly at anything for support. The roaring was more powerful down here, the cold so intense she shook violently from head to toe.

'Liza!' The shout from above snapped her to her senses.

'Robert, st...stay where you are. I'm knee-deep in water. The house is...is flooded!'

He cursed, violently; cursed again as he thumped the light-switch.

'The power's off!' she cried, her legs cramping painfully. The sudden thought of the coupling of water and electricity spurred her to scrabble, ter-rified, up the stairs. She cried out as Robert reached for her, and with a sob she fell into his arms, bringing them both crashing against the banister.

She blacked out for a second or two, and came round, shaking with shock and relief.

'Easy, Liza, I'm here. You're safe.' He held her tightly and she clung to him, burying her icy face in the warmth of his towelling robe.

He scooped her up and carried her up the re-maining stairs and across the landing. He lowered her down on to a bed. She clung to him, petrified and so terribly cold.

'You're soaked through,' he grated, and stripped her sopping gown over her head. Then he gathered her hard against him, his warmth breathing life into her. He lay with her on the bed, pulling the warm duvet around them both, till gradually her shaking eased and her brain started to function again.

'W... what happened?' she moaned weakly.

'I'm not sure.' He eased away from her and went to the window. Liza heard him moan.

'Stay where you are,' he said roughly and went to the door.

'Where are you going?' she cried, sitting up. It was getting light and she could see now.

'Downstairs.'

She scrambled out of bed when he'd gone, clutched the duvet round her and rushed to the window, for the first time realising she was in his bedroom not her own.

'Oh, my God!' she breathed with a catch of anxiety in her throat. Water! Everywhere. Nothing but water. The landscape as far as she could see was flooded with swirling muddy water. His bedroom faced the same way as hers—she recognised the big oak outside her window. Where the lake began and ended was beyond her.

'Has the lake overflowed?' she asked as he burst back into the room, stripping his robe from his back.

Liza looked away, heard him throwing open the wardrobe. When she raised her eyes he was struggling into jeans.

'Robert, what's happened?' she cried.

'Get back into bed,' he rasped. 'You were right: the house is flooded, the whole area is under water. I'd imagine the river across the meadow has burst its banks, and the reservoir, *and* the damned lake!'

It was getting lighter by the minute and Liza could see the whiteness of his face.

'But this is England!' she blurted. 'Berkshire...' Her voice trailed away. What a stupid thing to say when it was there before her eyes.

Robert thought the same as he grunted and ordered her back into bed.

'There's nothing you can do and you've had a nasty shock. You're half-frozen as well. Keep warm.' Pulling a thick sweater over his head, he lifted the receiver of the phone by the bed. 'The phone's out too,' he raged, slamming it down. He stormed out of the room.

She understood his anger and dismay. His beautiful house and his trees and shrubs would all be ruined by the flood water. And, worse, how would they ever get out of here? They were trapped!

Liza ran to her room and pulled on her jogging-suit bottoms. They were warmer than jeans and stretched up over her knees. The top she cast aside as too flimsy. She was still cold, bitterly so.

She hurried back to Robert's room and took a thick sweater from his wardrobe and huddled into it. Then she went to the stairs and looked down.

She'd never witnessed such a sight in her life before and her hand came up to her mouth to stem the cry that came to her lips. Murky brown water swirled around the small mahogany hall-table, lapped up the walls, soaked up the drapes of the windows at the side of the front door. A rug was caught against the stairs and Liza ran down and rescued it. It was Persian and weighty with mud and water, but with a supreme effort she hauled it up over the banister.

'I thought I told you to stay in bed!' Robert shouted from the kitchen. He waded towards her, knee deep, water soaked into his jeans up to his thighs.

'Don't be ridiculous! I can't lie there and do nothing.' She stepped down into the water, her feet sinking into sludge. She remembered the electricity. 'Is there a chance of electrocution if the power comes on again?' she asked warily.

'I've switched it off from the mains anyway. I think there's more chance of our drowning than anything.'

His feeble attempt at a joke fell on deaf ears. Liza struggled with the small table, trying to lift it.

'What the hell do you think you're doing?' he bellowed at her.

'If we can get most of the furniture upstairs——'

'Don't be bloody ridiculous,Liza. The stuff's insured anyway!'

'*You're* being ridiculous!' Liza stormed back. 'They're antiques. No money in the world can compensate for their loss. You can't just let them be ruined like this. Come on, give me a hand.'

With a resigned growl he waded over to help her with the table. Together they manhandled it on to the stairs, where Robert took over and lifted it up on to the landing.

Liza went for the curtains and knotted them high above the water-line. She tried to open a door off the hall but the carpets had swollen and she couldn't budge it. Robert came to her rescue and forced it open. Water from a higher level in the hall powered into the once elegant sitting-room.

'That was stupid. We've made it worse now.'

'Only a matter of time before it would have seeped through.' Liza told him sensibly.

Together they stacked what they could on the window-seats of the two bay windows, both moving in a frenzy of shock and disbelief. Liza tied up the drapes and then they moved to the dining-room and did all they could there.

Robert's study was a scene of such destruction that Liza felt tears of despair prick her eyes. A bookcase had collapsed and books floated on the water. Soundlessly they moved, bobbing against each other. The glass in the french windows leading to the garden had smashed with the force

of the water and the room was open to the devas-
tating elements.

The roaring had stopped now, the silence
seeming to heighten the tragedy.

Liza looked at Robert, her heart aching for
him. This was his home, his country retreat,
where he'd gathered his most valued belongings.
His face was pale and gaunt, and if ever she'd
thought he was hard and unemotional she now
knew that not to be true. He turned away from
the devastation and waded back to the hall. There
was another room, a smaller sitting-room. Liza
sloshed after him, stood in the doorway and
watched him move towards the conservatory that
opened off it.

She was stunned by the colour and beauty that
filled the domed Victorian construction. Purple
and pink and white blooms contrasted so vividly
with the filthy brown water lapping the base of
the elegant standard fuchsias that she wanted to
cry with the pain of it.

She followed him through into the glass room,
shivering with the rapidly cooling humidity that
swamped her. She didn't know much about the
beautiful exotica that bloomed so stunningly, but
she did know that they needed warmth in winter.
She saw orchids too, pale fragile blooms that even
now seemed to be suffering from the dropping
temperature.

Liza reached for Robert's arm but before she
could offer any words of comfort he reached out
jerkily for a pot of vermilion geraniums. He

hurled the pot across the room with a roar of anguish. It smashed through a pane of glass and the terrible silence that followed was worse than his despaired roar and the shattering of glass.

'I'm sorry, Robert,' she offered weakly. What else could she say?

'So am I,' he grated and took her hand to lead her away. 'You're frozen. Come on, let's try to get out of here.'

'How can we? You've seen the water out there. We'll never get the car out.'

They heard pounding at the back door. 'Sounds like the cavalry,' Robert said with renewed hope in his voice.

'Robert, are you all right?' a deep voice thundered as a ruddy face pressed hard against the glass panel in the back door.

Robert heaved open the back door and a giant of a man in thigh-length waders sloshed in, dumping a camping stove and a spare container of gas on the work-service.

'Brought you these; you're going to need them, I'm afraid. I saw lights last night so thought you must be down for the weekend. Struth! You're in a worse state than we are,' he stated, looking around at the water in the kitchen.

'What's happening, Jack? What do you know?' Robert asked in a gravelly voice.

'The rain's stopped, if that's any consolation.' He stopped at the sight of Liza.

Briefly, Robert made the introductions. 'My neighbour, Jack Simmons; lives at the manor along the lane. Have you any communications, Jack? The phone's off here.'

'Same at my place. I'd say the whole area is out. The river burst its banks some years back and we just had to sit tight till the level dropped. We had no power for days. Sorry to be the bearer of more bad news, but the roads are impassable even if you managed to start your car.'

Robert raked a hand through his tousled hair. 'I can't afford days marooned here. I'd summon a helicopter if there were anywhere for the damned thing to land. You haven't got a dinghy by any chance?' he asked ruefully.

Jack shook his head. 'Can't even help in that direction, I'm afraid. Have you food and bottled water? I wouldn't chance the water supply.'

'Plenty; that's not a problem. Thanks for the stove, Jack. It was thoughtful of you.'

'I didn't think you'd have one,' Jack laughed. 'Hardly the camping type, are you? I'll be off now. Just wanted to check that you were all right. I'm wading down the lane to see if old Mrs Dowling is OK; she's on her own and more than likely terrified.'

'Let me know if there's anything I can do,' Robert offered.

Jack shook his head. 'Thanks for the offer, but look after yourselves. The young lady doesn't look too well.'

She doesn't feel too well, Liza groaned inside. She stared bleakly at Robert after his neighbour had left.

'It's like a nightmare,' Liza whispered, and then her whole body started to shake from her head to her very numb toes. She'd given no thought to her physical discomfort while they had been saving the furniture; now she ached with the cold and felt dizzy and sick.

'Come on, heroine. It's into a hot bath for you. You look like a half-drowned rat.' He scooped her up into his arms and carried her upstairs and set her down in his bedroom.

'We're going to have to camp out in this room for a while, I'm afraid.' He laughed at her bleak expression. 'We need each other's body warmth. No heating, no light . . .'

'And no hot water,' she added, the thought of a good hot soak rapidly diminishing.

'There'll be enough left in the tank for a couple of much needed baths,' he told her. 'We'll face tomorrow when it comes. While you thaw out I'll bring what we need up from the kitchen.'

He left her in the middle of the room, wet, cold and stunned by the turn of events. They couldn't live in this room together, marooned for possibly days, as Robert's neighbour had suggested. Liza staggered into Robert's bathroom, her legs weak and blue with cold. The water that gushed from the tap was hot but she was sparing with it, considering Robert's needs.

Considering Robert's needs, her mind echoed as she lowered herself into the warm water. Did he expect her to share his bed too? 'We need each other's body warmth,' he'd said. What more would he need?

She didn't want to cry, fought it desperately, but she'd had too many shocks to stop the flow. She buried her face in her hands and let the tears come.

'Hey, what's this?' Robert said softly.

Her head jerked up and her first thought was her nakedness. She clutched her arms around her breasts.

'Don't do that, Liza,' he told her quietly. 'You have nothing to fear from me.' He took a towel from the airing-cupboard behind him and, gently bringing her to her feet, he wrapped it around her and lifted her out of the bath. He held her against him, his warm, comforting lips pressed against her forehead.

'And there was I, thinking you were such a heroine, but you're nothing but a soft weak lamb,' he murmured against her.

'I've done nothing heroic,' she sobbed against his sweater.

'You gave me strength when I needed it. I'd say that was pretty heroic. You helped me save my furniture. I can't think of another woman in the world who would have been caring enough to do that. And now you are weak and exhausted and it's my turn to give you strength.'

'I...I'm all right.' She stifled back a sob, swallowed hard and braved herself to look up into his face. 'I am,' she assured him with a watery smile.

He looked down at her, his face grave and impassive. 'I believe you.' He smoothed her flame hair from her forehead, frowned as she winced and drew back. 'What's this, a bump?'

'I got up for a drink. It was dark and I walked into the wall.'

He laughed and drew her back into his arms. She playfully thumped his chest with her fist bunched with towelling. 'It's not funny! And then I went downstairs and fell in the water.'

His body shook with laughter against hers, till she too started to laugh, and then the laughter stopped abruptly. His mouth sought hers, feverishly. Was it the weakening effect of the tragic events of the morning, the shocks and the cold, that had her parting her lips to his so willingly? She returned his passion, every wild pulsing second of it, wriggled her arms free from the towel and slid them around his neck. His lips were unrelenting, almost savage in their need. Yes, it was a need, the one she had dreaded from him. But, worse, much worse, it was her need too. She wanted him, wanted him to make love to her to ease the pain of what had happened.

With an impassioned groan, an almost unwilling sound, drawn from deep within him, he moved the towel away from her body, and smoothed his hand over her breast. Liza trembled against him, cried out as his mouth lowered to her nipple and he ran his tongue lightly over it. Her body arched, an instinctive movement she couldn't have controlled if she'd tried. It affected him deeply, excited him to draw hard on her sensitive flesh. A deep *frisson* of wild need pulsed through every nerve and settled and pounded in her groin, a sweet pleasurable ache that demanded more and more.

His mouth came back to hers, tasted her sweetness, drew hard on her moistness. And then, as abruptly as the assault on her senses started, it ended. With a shudder that racked through his body he drew back from her.

Liza looked up at him, her green eyes wide and innocent, not understanding.

'We need to talk this out,' he grated roughly. He pulled the towel back round her shoulders.

Embarrassment suddenly flushing her cheeks, she stepped back from him. Her brain wouldn't function her lips to work. She just stood there, weak and vulnerable, not knowing what to do or say.

He made decisions for her, ordered her gently but firmly to get dressed. She faltered, her words coming halted and uncertain.

'I ... I don't ... my clothes, they're wet.' Her mind started to clear. She hadn't bought suitable clothes for a siege such as this. Her velvet jogging-suit was ruined, her jeans cold ...

Robert left her, and came back with one of his thick tracksuits, a black one with 'Claudio' printed on the front.

'Get into this; it's big and warm, and I have plenty for the two of us.' His tone, gentle and persuasive, urged her into it. He went back into

the bedroom for thick socks, which she pulled
on to her feet.

'I've set up the stove. Could you make some
coffee while I bring the rest of the stuff up?'

She nodded, not able to meet his gaze. She
tidied the bathroom when he'd gone, draped her
wet clothes over the cold radiator, and cleaned
the bath for him. She did it mechanically, moving
as if she were programmed by something other
than her own brain. Then she went out to the
bedroom.

While she had been whimpering in the bath
Robert had worked like a Trojan. The camping
stove was set up on a round table by the window.
He'd placed two of the kitchen chairs round the
hall table. They could eat there, Liza supposed;
work too. Work? How could they possibly carry
on? Robert obviously thought so. The paperwork they had left spread on the kitchen table
was now piled on the window seat.

For the first time Liza gazed properly round
the room. There were redwood fitted wardrobes,
a huge bed with a headboard carved in matching
wood, a dusky-blue silk upholstered chesterfield
and a matching armchair, both more for decor-
ative purposes than use. The pale ochre carpet
was thick and warm, and on the whole the room
was comfortable enough for a sit-in. They would
survive, Liza thought, but could they survive
what was nagging deep inside her? That need they
had both expressed so openly in the bathroom.

And yet he had pulled back from her, he the one to stop it going any further.

Liza filled a pan with two measured mugs of bottled water and lit the stove, adjusting the flame to conserve the energy. She watched the tiny bubbles forming inside the pan. She didn't want to think beyond those bubbles but she had to, forced herself to.

Would he regret his constraint and try again? If he did, it was going to take an iron will to prevent it going further. While they were cooped up here the strain was going to be enormous. She looked out of the window at the grey clouds heavy in the sky, the swirling brown water that stretched for miles. She'd never experienced anything like this before, stranded in a flooded house with a man. Not just any man either. Robert Buchanan, a very attractive, sexual man with a weakness for redheads. She closed her eyes and bit her lip.

'I think that's the lot.' He heaved a box of groceries and a silver candelabrum on to the bed.

Liza stared at the candelabrum. Dark nights, candlelight. Her worrying thoughts had got her no further than the long days ahead. The nights had to be survived too!

'I'll take my bath while the water boils. There are some cereals and the last of the fresh milk for breakfast.' He smiled at the look of dismay on her face. 'Cheer up, Liza. It could be worse. You could be stuck here with Frankenstein's monster instead of me.'

'I see no difference,' she shot back dismally.

'That's better,' he grinned. 'You're getting your sense of humour back.' He slammed the bathroom door after him, proving to Liza that he hadn't been at all amused by her remark.

Was he a two-Weetabix man? she wondered as she opened the packet. How little she knew of him. But by the time the flood-tide receded she would know all, almost all. She wouldn't know if he was a good lover or mediocre because she wasn't going to allow a repeat of what had happened in the bathroom. She smiled. Was she trying to fool herself? *He* had been the one to cool off. He wouldn't try again. He just wouldn't!

She set two cereal bowls out on the table. The water was taking an age to boil and she made the bed while she waited. She called out to him when the coffee was ready.

He came out of the bathroom almost immediately, dressed in the black tracksuit he'd worn the night before.

'Do you feel OK?' he asked, sitting across from her.

'I'm warm at last,' she offered, drinking her coffee thirstily. In the trauma of finding the ground floor flooded she had forgotten the purpose of the trip downstairs. Pity she couldn't forget so easily everything that had happened since.

'Loosen up, Liza. This is a difficult situation for the two of us. I'm as shocked at the predicament we're in as you are.'

Her eyes pleaded with his. 'Is it hopeless? Isn't there any way we can get out of here?'

'I haven't got wings and I don't know Superman personally——'

'For Christ's sake, can't you take this seriously?' she blazed at him.

'I am taking it seriously. No, there is no way out of here,' he told her firmly.

He finished his cereal and leaned back in the chair to drink his coffee. 'I'm sorry, Liza, sorry I ever brought you here. But the fact is, it's happened. You and I are stranded and we'll just have to suffer each other till the water goes down and the roads are passable. I don't like it any more than you do, and don't look hurt. I don't mean it personally. Come Monday morning, I'm going to be as sick as hell if we are still here without any communication with the outside world. I have a business to run, and one day without me at the helm——'

'You're not indispensable!' she interrupted.

'No, I'm not,' he agreed with a sigh. 'Nevertheless I don't want to be here any longer than is necessary.'

'I don't want to be here at all!' she snapped. 'I wish we'd never come!' She let out a long sigh of despair; rubbed at her forehead. 'I'm sorry, that was childish of me.'

'Very, and that's why we've got to talk this out. We're going to be living in a vacuum, and it's best we get our feelings out into the open and not waste our time and energy trying to cut each other's throats.'

With a deep breath Liza calmed herself. 'You're right.' She gave a shrug. 'After all, we came here to work, and what difference does it make if we work downstairs or up here?'

'The difference is that we are going to have to eat and sleep here as well. In this room, together.'

'I'll sleep in my own room——'

'You'll do as you're told.'

Her eyes warred with his. 'I'm not sleeping in that bed with you!' she cried vehemently.

'Be sensible, Liza. The rain has stopped and the temperature has dropped considerably. This is a big old house and there is no heating, no light. If we stay in this room we'll be all right. I'll sleep on the floor if you want——'

'You won't!' she insisted. 'You'll sleep in your own bed and I'll sleep in mine. I'll put some extra blankets on the bed——'

'Anything but curl up next to me in mine?'

'You know what would happen if we did!' It was out before she could stop it, those few words that indicated the deep anxiety inside her.

'I know exactly what would happen,' he said solemnly. 'We would make love. All night and every night we were here.'

'Well, you're honest,' she snorted with a smile of derision on her lips.

'Wipe that smirk off your face and be honest with me, then.' His tone was deadly serious, and Liza levelled her eyes at him. This situation was intolerable, but they were two intelligent people who should be able to work this out reasonably and sensibly.

'I don't know if I can,' she whispered, averting her eyes to the window. How could she tell him how she felt? How afraid she was?

'Shall I make it easier for you? Tell you what I think and let you take it from there?'

She didn't answer, but stared bleakly out at grey and more grey.

'I think you want me as much as I want you; at least, that is what you led me to believe in the bathroom earlier.'

'If you know so much you don't need me to admit it, then.'

'I do; I want to hear you say it and I'd like you to look at me while you do.'

'You're asking the impossible, Robert,' she smoothed. 'Women can't admit to that sort of thing.'

'The women I mix with do, invariably so.'

'I'm not one of those women. I'm not a Lady Victoria.'

'And I'm not a Graham. I wouldn't hurt you,' he said softly.

She looked at him then. 'Could you guarantee that?' she asked sharply.

It was his turn to look away, unable to hold her gaze. He stood up and walked to the window, his back to her when he spoke. 'Is that what all this is about? If we make love you want my undying love?'

'I didn't say that.'

'You mean it, though.'

'I don't!' she insisted heatedly. 'Don't forget it was you who pulled back. If you want my honesty here it is: yes, I wanted you, and if I'm forced to share your bed I can't guarantee I won't want you again. But we're not animals, you know, we just can't do it and then amble off into the bush somewhere and never see each other again. I work for you. We're going to see each other every day of our working lives. We've been forced together in this unique situation where emotions are sure to run high.' She stood up, trembling. 'It would be so easy for us to give in and make love—because of who you are you probably think it's inevitable—but we only need each other because everything around us is so...so bloody! Next week you'll not give me a thought, and what am I left with? You say you wouldn't hurt me, but how do I know I won't fall in love with you?'

He turned then and the pain in his eyes shook her.

'And I suppose it's never occurred to you that the same applies to me,' he said quietly and with such deep meaning her stomach knotted.

Her mouth was so dry she swallowed hard before she could speak. 'I don't believe you. You're just saying that to make it easier for yourself, perhaps to lower my resistance.' She shook her head determinedly. 'No, I'm not going to take that risk, Robert. I don't want it, don't need it! I'm going to get out of here, breast-stroke or whatever, but I'm not staying to be used and humiliated!'

With that she turned and ran from the room, slammed into her bedroom, and started to pull on her shoes. She'd get away from him somehow. About that she was determined!

CHAPTER FIVE

'LIZA, be sensible. You can't get out of here. You don't even know where you are.' Robert took her overnight bag from her hands and threw it down on the floor.

Anger and frustration zapped out of her, leaving her exhausted. Her shoulders slumped in defeat.

'You're right,' she murmured. 'I don't know where I am, but I just can't accept that there's no hope.'

'I understand how you feel,' he said softly, an arm sliding around her shoulder in comfort. 'It's an awful situation and I'm not making it easier for you.'

She let him lead her back into his bedroom, which she had to admit was much warmer than her own, sat her down on the bed and eased off her shoes.

Liza drew her legs up and sat cross-legged on the bed. She was going to be sensible, try to be reasonable. It *was* an intolerable situation, but one they could do nothing about. Yet if they controlled their emotions they could come through it.

'I'm sorry I said all those silly things,' she breathed unevenly. She felt foolish now. Her outburst had revealed too much of her inner self.

'They weren't silly at all. It's how you feel.' He sat at the table to finish his coffee. 'But I have feelings too, you know. It angers me to think you class me with your former lover. He hurt you, so you suppose every other man will too. I'm not him and you're not like any other woman. We are two separate people at this moment, divided from the outside world.'

'In other words, what goes on here is irrelevant to what goes on out there? You don't mind an affair so long as it doesn't interfere with the rest of your life? Would that it could be that easy!' she said ruefully.

'So do I. I'm as terrified of falling in love as you are.'

She looked at him in surprise, missing the point that she might be the one if he did. 'Have you been hurt too?'

'Not yet, but it's always a possibility, isn't it? The world is full of hurt, rejected people. I don't want to be one of them. I live life to the full. I'm ambitious, just like you. I love my work and I'm free to travel and pursue my life in the way I want.'

'And use women on the way?'

'You're the first woman who has ever suggested that. I've never seen it that way, nor have the women I've known. In spite of what the Press say about me I'm not Bluebeard. I have a lot of women friends. I like women. I don't bed all of them.'

'Just the ones you need at the time.' She looked away from him. She'd thought he might be different but he wasn't.

'Everyone needs someone. I'm not celibate, but I don't use and humiliate women as you suppose I do. I have an enormous respect for them, probably, if I really tried to analyse it, the reason why I don't get too deeply involved. I haven't much to offer a woman. Material things, yes, but like yours, my heart is something else. I'm not sure I could love anyone enough to offer myself for life.'

'It's the commitment that terrifies you?'

'Probably. I've never given it much thought. I just can't see me bouncing babies on my lap.'

Liza smiled reluctantly. 'Nor can I.'

'And what about you?' he grinned. 'Is that what you want?'

'Babies? Marriage?' She shook her head, pushed her hair from her face. 'I honestly don't know,' she admitted. 'I thought I wanted marriage to Graham, but babies never came into it. I never thought beyond living together, with him writing and me pursuing my own career. Maybe that was why I failed. I was giving off negative currents. Graham needed a family life and I was always wanting to go out to the theatre or something. You're right, it wouldn't have worked for us.'

'But what about marriage to someone else?'

Liza shrugged. 'I don't know any more. I suppose the hurt is easing a bit, but I love working for Magnum. For the first time in my life I'm stimulated. I don't think I could give that up.'

He laughed. 'So here we are, two dedicated ambitious people, heading for the biggest downfall of our lives.'

Liza's head jerked up, her eyes widened. 'What do you mean?' she rasped.

'Neither of us wants to fall in love, and yet here we are, forced to spend every second in each other's company in this room, with sexual awareness of each other rebounding off the walls.'

Quelling her rising temperature, she stated flatly, 'Sex, not love. Two very different things.'

'But you were right. We aren't animals. We have feelings.'

'*I* have feelings. You are determined not to fall in love and it would be me who suffered if we let our emotions rule our heads.'

'I'm not so sure about that,' he said gravely. 'You should see yourself sitting there. Scrubbed and innocent with your flame hair frizzed around your lovely face. You have a Renaissance beauty that any man would kill for——'

'Shut up!' Liza snapped, swinging her legs to the floor.

'There's nowhere to run, Liza,' he grated. 'But don't worry, I've no intention of trying to persuade you to do anything you don't want to do. If we do lapse it will come from you, not me. You won't find me an unwilling lover. On that note I think we'll conclude this line of conversation and get on with some work.'

It was the most sensible suggestion she'd heard so far. Well, at least he'd put the ball in her court. She didn't have to share his bed if she didn't want to. Nothing could be easier!

Liza cleared the breakfast things and rinsed them in the bathroom, then went back to the bedroom and sat across from him.

They worked for a couple of hours, making notes and discussing forthcoming projects and how it would affect the advertising Liza and her team would have to pull in. Liza was so absorbed she didn't hear the helicopter overhead till Robert went to the window.

'What is it?' she said, joining him.

Robert slid the heavy sash windows up and they both leaned out.

'Looks like a police helicopter.' He leaned out further and waved. The helicopter circled, came down lower. 'At least they know we are here and safe.' He waved an acknowledgement and the pilot and his passenger waved back and then swooped away, banking sharply and speeding off over the wet landscape.

'They might have lowered a ladder or something and got us out of here,' Liza commented ruefully as Robert slid the window down.

'I expect there are more deserving cases. There's a cottage hospital in the area and I should imagine there's chaos there if it's cut off by the floods.'

That's me in my place, Liza thought. And rightly so. She hadn't given a thought to anyone else. At least they were warm and dry and had plenty of supplies.

They carried on working till hunger overcame them both. There was some casserole left over from the night before, and Liza added a can of oxtail soup to make it go further and set the pan on the small stove to heat it through. Robert cut up the last of the fresh bread his housekeeper had brought. There was more in the freezer.

They worked as they ate because Robert pointed out that they had to take advantage of the light.

'I don't know why I didn't think of it before,' he said suddenly, 'but I've a portable radio around somewhere. I might be able to pick up the local station and find out what's going on. I'll check to see if the water level is dropping while I'm down there.'

'I'll make some coffee,' Liza said, stretching her long legs.

She cleared the dishes, glad to be able to move around and do something other than pore over papers for hours on end. It seemed to be getting colder, and she shivered as she worked. The water in the bathroom was cold now and added to the misery. She warmed her hands on the stove as she waited for the water to boil for coffee.

'Any change?' she asked hopefully when Robert returned, his tracksuit bottoms pulled up over his knees.

'None, but at least the weather forecast isn't all gloom and despondency. No more rain coming, but high winds forecast for tonight.'

'I suppose it could be worse.' Liza tried to sound cheerful.

'The wind might push over the trees that have had their roots weakened by all this water, though,' Robert stated despondently.

'I hadn't thought of that.' She looked at Robert seated on the window seat, twiddling the knobs of an ancient portable. He tuned in to some pop music which lightened the atmosphere a bit. 'I'm really sorry about all this,' she said quietly. 'It must be awful for you, seeing your lovely house ruined, all your fuchsias suffering so.'

'Some of them might survive; those that don't are replaceable,' he said curtly, and she knew the abruptness of his tone hid his true feelings. 'My father would go to pieces if he were here,' he went on. 'He grows orchids up in Scotland, has three greenhouses full of them. He gave me my love of exotica. My mother paints them. Exhibits her work all over the world.'

'I've seen them!' Liza exclaimed in surprise. 'Marion Buchanan. She had an exhibition in Kensington last year.'

Robert lifted his head and smiled. 'It's a wonder we didn't bump into each other. I was there several times.' He talked about his parents and Liza listened while they drank their coffee. She was learning something new about him all the time, liking something new about him too, which disturbed her. Funny how the Press always got hold of the bad bits—his ruthlessness in business, his conquests with women. He was obviously devoted to his talented parents and had inherited a lot of their passions, but that sort of information didn't sell papers. Redheads and power struggles did.

'What's that?' Liza shot up and went to the window. 'Another helicopter.'

Robert hauled open the window again and they both leaned out.

It was a helicopter, but not the same one as earlier. It was smaller and hovered above the rooftop then swung away, coming down lower and seemingly to pass feet from the open window. Liza laughed and covered her ears, the noise of the blades deafening her and the current swirling her hair around her face.

To her surprise Robert pulled her back from the window and slammed it shut with such force that the glass panes shuddered in their frame.

'Sightseers,' he said roughly. 'Some people will do anything for kicks.'

'It was awfully close,' Liza gasped, trying to sort out her hair, which was a wild mass around her head. 'I thought it was going to hit the oak tree.'

'Pity it didn't!' Robert snapped, and, surprised, Liza turned to look at him. His eyes were dark with anger, his jaw set tightly. She was about to ask what was wrong, but he sat down at the table, and started to leaf through papers, and the words died on her lips.

They worked for another couple of hours till the failing light made it difficult to concentrate.

'I think it's time to stop,' Robert said with a glance at his watch. 'It will be completely dark shortly.' He stood up and drew the curtains across the window to keep in the heat. Of which there wasn't very much, Liza thought ruefully. The atmosphere felt damp too, rising from downstairs no doubt.

'You're cold,' Robert observed. 'Slip a sweater over your top. Are you hungry yet?'

Liza shook her head. 'Not really. Have you another sweater I can borrow?' She laughed. 'I'm going through your wardrobe as if there were no tomorrow.'

He threw her one from the wardrobe. 'Well, there is a tomorrow and we're going to get out of here if it kills us.' He said it with such conviction that Liza frowned. He'd seemed preoccupied this afternoon and she didn't know why. Nothing had changed, but maybe this enforced confinement was beginning to get at him.

She watched him as he put candles in the candelabrum and lit them. He lit another and took it to the bathroom. 'Do you want to freshen up?'

So she looked that bad? Well he didn't look too smart either—his hair was rumpled and his face was darker than ever with five o'clock shadow.

'Yes, I would,' she admitted. 'I'll get my toiletries from my room.'

She was shocked at the coldness that assailed her as she opened the door of her bedroom. The forecast wind had started and was rattling the ill-fitting window-frames. There was enough light to grab her toilet bag by. She pulled the curtains across the window before she hurried back to Robert's room. It was going to be like trying to sleep in a mausoleum tonight.

She washed her face in Robert's bathroom and forced a comb through her mass of unruly hair and felt better for the effort; warmer too. Robert was boiling water when she went back into the bedroom.

'This stove generates quite a bit of heat. If the worst comes to the worst we can huddle round it later.'

'It smells, though.' Liza wrinkled her nose. 'You'll never sleep tonight with the fumes.'

'Don't you mean *we'll* never sleep?' he said with a smile, the first she'd seen on his face all afternoon.

'My room isn't so bad,' Liza lied, her heart beating warily. She didn't want him to start that all over again. 'With extra blankets I'm sure I'll sleep like a top.'

He made no comment at that, and Liza was glad that at last he'd accepted that she wasn't going to share his bed with him.

'No work tonight. I think we've had enough for one day. I suggest a warming cup of coffee now, a game of cards, and later I'll cook us a couple of steaks. We have the radio, and you never know your luck—there might be a good play on later.'

Liza agreed. It was going to be a long evening and an even longer night, but it was going to be all right. They were coping.

Later, after Robert had thrashed her at gin rummy and the batteries in the radio had given out, Liza insisted on cooking the steaks that Robert had taken out of the freezer that morning. She tossed in a tin of potatoes to make a meal.

'Looked ghastly but tasted divine,' Robert said with a grin, putting his knife and fork down on his empty plate.

'I suppose half a compliment is better than none,' she smiled, leaning back in her chair. She'd spent most of the day in this chair. It was stiff and unyielding and she longed to flop out somewhere.

'As you insisted on cooking the meal I'll do the washing-up.' Robert got up and took the plates to the bathroom.

Liza yawned and looked at her watch. There was really no need to stay up any longer, no point. She gazed round the room, still not quite believing what had happened. The candles were guttering low, casting soft shadows round the room. Cooking the food in here had certainly helped to keep it warm, but nevertheless it was an unwelcome prison and the thought of several more days of not being able to wash properly, improvising meals, and not being able to go for a walk to relieve her aching limbs, was a depressing thought. But hadn't Robert said he was going to try to get out of here if it killed him? The freedom of the sightseers in that helicopter must have affected him. It was worse for him, she reasoned, a man in his position trapped with one of his employees.

She went to the bathroom. 'Would you mind very much if I went to bed?' She smiled at him scrubbing the greasy plates in the bathroom sink. 'I wish I had a camera to record this: *the* Robert Buchanan, washing up by candlelight.'

He grinned. 'Not in character, is it?'

'On the contrary, I think it suits you.' Liza laughed. 'Goodnight, Robert.'

'Goodnight, Liza. Take a candle and matches with you and don't forget the extra blankets. Top of the wardrobe. Let's hope everything looks brighter in the morning.'

It was as easy as that. Liza glowed with a sense of achievement. She was coping and so was he. It wasn't going to be as bad as she'd imagined.

She went to bed and tried to sleep, curled under the extra blankets in Robert's tracksuit, and tried to generate heat, but it was impossible. The wind was violent now and howled and rattled the windows till she nearly cried in despair. She supposed she must have fallen asleep, for a sudden vicious howl of wind jolted her aching limbs alive. The bathroom door wasn't closed properly and was banging, and Liza got up to shut it.

Before she could crawl back into bed the whole house seemed to shake. There was a terrible noise, shuddering and grating, and then what sounded like an explosion in the room, so loud and terrifying that Liza screamed with fear. Glass fell all around her and the raw wind howled in her face. She let out a strangled sob as the floor came up to meet her.

She didn't know how long she had been unconscious, but when her head cleared and she opened her eyes Robert was with her. They were in his room and he was bathing her forehead with a wet towel.

'It's OK, you're safe.'

She'd heard those words before. It was a nightmare, repeating itself over and over again. She wasn't wet though, not this time, and she was comfortable enough, warm enough. She tried to sit up. Robert restrained her.

'This would never have happened if you'd done as I suggested.' His words were surprisingly harsh and angry. 'A branch from the oak crashed through your window.'

She remembered. The wind and the horrible grinding sound and then the explosion of breaking glass. But it hadn't been her fault; how could he blame her, how could he be angry with her?

'It landed on your bed—thank God you weren't in it! What were you doing the other side of the room?'

'The bathroom door was banging in the wind. I got up to close it.' She sat up, pushed his hands aside. 'Leave me alone! I'm all right!' She was angry at him for being angry with her. 'It wasn't my fault. I don't control the weather, you know!'

He let out a long-drawn-out sigh of resignation. 'I'm sorry I snapped at you, but I thought you were hurt——'

'Hurt! I could have been killed!' she cried in anguish.

'Yes, and that's why I'm so angry with you!' he snapped back irrationally. 'If you'd stayed here as I suggested you wouldn't have been in any danger. You gave me the fright of my life. I

heard the crash and rushed in to find a damned
tree across the bed where you should have been
lying, and you crumpled on the floor in a dead
faint! Now, for once in your life, listen to me.
In future you'll do as I say without any ridiculous arguments.' His voice suddenly softened, re-
gretting his outburst. 'I'll make you some tea.
Just lie there and get yourself together.'

Liza flung herself back on the pillows. How
dared he rage at her so? Given *him* the fright of
his life? How did he think *she* felt? She bit her
lip hopelessly. How blind of her. He was furious
because he felt responsible for her. It was his idea
to come here to work. None of this would have
happened if they'd worked the weekend in the
Magnum offices.

She heard a muttered curse from the bathroom
and what sounded like Robert pounding the taps.

'You're not going to believe this, but there's
no water,' he told her.

Believe it? She'd believe it if a mad elephant
rampaged into the room! She turned her face into
the pillow and let out a moan of anguish, and
beat her fists on the bedding.

'I can't take any more! I just want to get out
of here! It's like a house of horror! What next?
What next?' she sobbed.

Robert gathered her into his arms, cradled her
and her despair against him. 'My poor darling,'
he grated into her hair. 'You're frightened and
exhausted and I'm doing nothing to help you,

am I?' He smoothed her hair and held her hard against him.

Liza felt the slow beat of his heart next to her, heard the wind raging relentlessly outside. She felt safe and warm in his arms; protected. It wasn't his fault and yet she was blaming him, acting like a spoiled child. Biting her lower lip resolutely, she clung to him.

'I'm sorry, sorry for not being stronger. Your poor house, and me nothing but trouble. Forgive me, Robert. I'm being selfish. I understand how you feel responsible for me...'

'Responsible?' he laughed wryly. 'Oh, my love, it's more than that, much more.'

She tried to raise her flushed face to his, not understanding, but he stilled her with his hand, held her head against his chest and caressed her hair. They didn't move for a long while, but lay in each other's arms while the storm raged and tore outside. Then Robert unwound her arms from his waist and moved off the bed. Liza curled in a ball on her side and watched him in the candlelight, watched him fill the pan with bottled water. Even against the raging backdrop of the storm she was acutely aware of rustling as he opened a packet of tea-bags, of the gentle hiss of the camping stove. The light from the blue flames and the candles on the table accentuated his drawn features, and she thought how very tired and exhausted he looked. And yet there he was, brewing tea for her at God only knew what time of the night.

In that moment she wanted to go to him, to touch him and comfort him. In that same moment she knew she was lost. Her eyes blurred with tears at the realisation that she loved him. But strangely, very strangely, they were not tears of hopelessness but more of relief. She felt that a battle was over, not fought and won, but surrendered, unconditionally. Maybe it was better this way, to love him and admit it to herself instead of battling with this inner turmoil. The pain and anguish would come later, of that she was sure, because it was a hopeless love. But for now the acceptance of it was a step forward, something positive to work towards overcoming.

'I've put plenty of sugar in,' he said quietly, handing her a mug of tea as she sat up and leaned back against the headboard. 'They say it's good for shock.'

'Thank you,' she said softly and took it from his hand.

'You're looking more relaxed now. Do you feel better?'

She nodded. They drank their tea in silence, Liza propped against the headboard, Robert perched on the edge of the bed. When they had finished he took the mug from her and got up. Liza slid down the bed, warmth and sleepiness overcoming her. Through half-closed eyes she watched him put the mugs down on the table and move the curtains aside to gaze out into darkness. He was still standing there when her lids closed completely.

*　　*　　*

Liza awoke the next morning, warmer and more comfortable than she had felt for a long time. Light came through the gap in the curtains where Robert had stood in the night.

He lay beside her now, his breathing even and regular, indicating he was still deep in sleep. One arm was thrown across her protectively. Liza didn't move a muscle for fear of disturbing him. They were both fully clothed under the duvet.

Liza smiled. How easily he could have loved her in the night. She wouldn't have turned away from him. She had been weak and vulnerable then, and that wouldn't have been right, so she was happy that he hadn't pressured her into something she would regret. Somehow it strengthened her love for him—his respect for her, and it was respect, she convinced herself. He'd admitted he wanted to make love to her, and the last twenty-four hours couldn't have changed that, but he had held back and she knew with certainty it was because he didn't want to hurt her.

Robert moved away from her to roll on to his back, taking his protective arm with him. Liza afforded herself a tentative stretch and then carefully slid out from under the duvet.

Her head ached with the stuffiness of the room and her mouth felt dry. While Robert slept she would wash and change her clothes and then start breakfast, but first she wanted to go to her room, to see the damage in the cold light of a new day.

Liza clutched at her chest when she saw the room, nausea filling her at the sight of the bed she had slept in, the bed she would have been crushed in if she hadn't been across the room shutting the bathroom door. The window had caved in and the brickwork above the shattered frame gaped open to the elements. The wind had not abated in the night and raged furiously around the room.

Liza stared, stupefied, at the bed. It had collapsed on to the floor with the weight of a huge gnarled branch of the tree, torn from the trunk as if it were nothing but a sapling. She had narrowly escaped death, and her heart raced urgently at the thought. No wonder Robert had been angry with her. He must have walked into this room and thought the very worst, that she was crushed under that branch, and all because of her own stupidity.

She walked from the room, her legs weak and shaky. She needed exercise. She decided to wander through the other rooms, curiosity and the need to stretch her legs spurring her on. There was no damage in the other five bedrooms. She wandered in each of them, pausing to look out of the windows. Robert's car, parked on lower ground, was in deeper water than the downstairs rooms. Beyond its axles in brown muddy water, it looked very forlorn and sorry for itself. With a shiver Liza inspected the other two bathrooms on the landing. She turned on the taps of a sink in one; water spurted unexpectedly and she plunged in the plug to save it. She supposed it was what was left in the pipes. It would be useful for washing in.

She went back to Robert's room, where he slept on, and picked up the pan, then went back and scooped up the water from the sink. Robert would need a shave.

While it heated on the stove she took a clean tracksuit from his wardrobe and went back to her own bathroom, where she found enough water left in the pipes to wash and clean her teeth. She combed through her hair and left it loose around her shoulders—it was warmer that way.

She had breakfast on the go when Robert finally stirred with a groan.

'Is that the way you normally come round in the mornings, like an angry bear?' She smiled across at him.

'Not normally, but then these aren't normal times, are they?' He stretched lazily and cupped his hands behind his head to look at her. 'Do you know you purr in your sleep, like a contented cat?'

'I was warm and cosy, I suppose. Two eggs? I think we should start the day with a good breakfast, don't you? I've boiled some water for your shave. It's in the bathroom by the sink.'

'Thanks, but I have an electric shaver,' he yawned.

'That should keep you well occupied all day, then!' Liza grinned.

Robert groaned. 'Did I really say that? I must be going mad.' He got up and staggered to the bathroom; two minutes later he called out for fresh clothes. Liza went to the wardrobe and dragged out a dark navy tracksuit, went to the chest of drawers and rummaged for clean underwear for him.

She laughed out loud when he emerged later, his chin covered in tiny pieces of tissue to stem the blood.

'I don't see what's so funny. You should try shaving with a blunt razor some time.'

'No, thanks, I'd rather grow a beard,' she joked back.

'You're different today,' he said as they sat down to breakfast—bacon, eggs, sliced bread and butter and mugs of hot coffee. 'Happier.'

'I'd call it resigned. We are stuck here and have to make the most of it; besides, I've got this stove off to a fine art now. It's a question of organisation. Shuffling pans and getting the timing right.'

'Sounds a good philosophy for life in general,' he returned with a grin.

'What, shuffling pans?'

'I was thinking more of getting the timing right,' he said, his voice loaded with innuendo.

A piece of bacon caught in Liza's throat. She gulped at her coffee to ease it. She knew exactly what he meant, it was as plain as the tissue on his grinning face. Oh, what an idiot she had been. He hadn't laid a finger on her all night, and why?

Because the timing hadn't been right, that was why! Nothing to do with respect for her wishes or not wanting to hurt her. Angry bear? He was more like the king of the jungle, biding his time till his prey was in sight!

Liza calmed her ragged nerves, reminding herself of her discovery that she was in love with this man. Even now, knowing he wasn't about to let up on her, she still cared deeply for him. Dangerous, she knew, but wasn't the jungle a treacherous place? The threatened outwitting the hunter was always a possibility, though.

She smiled. 'I understand what you're getting at,' she said softly, and her heart leapt at the sudden frown on his brow. She'd unnerved him for the moment. Would she be able to keep it up? Could she outdistance him on the flat? And a more disturbing thought: did she want to? It would be so easy to give in to temptation, to love him for this one weekend in her life. Knowing it could go no further didn't lessen the temptation. She'd get hurt again, but hadn't she fallen in love with Robert when she had vowed after Graham there would never be another?

Her thoughts shook her, and solemnly she went on with her breakfast. She didn't know herself any more, couldn't reason with herself any longer, but a decision would have to be made, some time soon. When the timing was right!

CHAPTER SIX

'A SMALL miracle!' Robert exclaimed, coming into the room as Liza was heating soup for their lunch.

'Don't tell me,' Liza laughed, 'you've chartered the *Ark Royal* to rescue us. It's steaming up the lane at this very moment!'

'I said a *small* miracle,' Robert grinned, coming to peer into the pan of vegetable soup that was on the stove.

Liza shrugged. 'OK, a pedalo, then.'

'Can't you be serious for a minute?'

'I think all this has gone to my head,' she said light-heartedly. 'I'm showing signs of mania. Now all our work has finished, what on earth are we going to do? I'm not playing rummy with you again, you cheat.'

They'd ploughed on with their paperwork all morning, and in a way Liza was glad it was over. It had occupied them fully, but now she was mentally tired. She longed to get out for some fresh air, but it was impossible of course.

'The water level downstairs is dropping.'

'What?' Liza shrieked with excitement, dropping the spoon into the soup and rushing to the window. During the morning the wind had dropped to little more than a breeze. Now a small glimmer of watery sun broke through the grey cloud. 'It doesn't look any different down there,' she observed gloomily. 'It must have been your imagination.'

'Come and see for yourself,' Robert suggested.

Liza turned down the soup and followed him downstairs, stopped on the last dry stair, and stared down. 'You're right. It's gone down an inch or two.' The dirty line on the wallpaper was clear to see.

'I'm going outside to look around. Maybe there is something we can do—dig some trenches to ease the flow of water away from the house, maybe.'

Well, she'd been complaining of lack of exercise. But digging trenches?

'Wait for me.' She started to roll up the legs of her tracksuit.

'Don't you dare!' Robert warned good-humouredly. 'Get back to the stove, woman. I'm not doing anything till I've assessed the situation.' He started to wade through to the kitchen, and Liza went back upstairs to rescue the soup before it burned.

Minutes later Robert came back, holding two pairs of wellington boots above his head in triumph. 'Found these in the gardener's shed. Miles too big for you, of course, but bearable with a few pairs of my socks to pad them out.'

With a smile of resignation, Liza dished up the soup. Robert was obviously as eager as herself for some physical exercise.

After they'd eaten she pulled layer upon layer of socks over her feet, and even then there was room for another foot in each enormous boot. Anything was better than sludge between her bare toes, though. Together they tramped outside, the water mercifully below the top of their boots.

'Look, if I dig a couple of trenches down to lower ground some of the water will drain away.'

'I'll try to sweep the water out of the house.' It might work, she supposed. Robert was already at work with a pick and shovel, his muscles bunching urgently under his sweater. She watched for a while, more fascinated by his physical form than the work he was doing. Then she turned away with a small sigh and went inside the house.

She found a broom in a cupboard in the kitchen and started urging the murky water outside. After a few minutes she shouted out, 'It's working!'

With renewed encouragement she sloshed through the rooms, opening all the doors and windows. The sun was desperately trying to break through and when she went back outside Robert looked up and smiled at her.

There was something in that smile that was unfathomable. Liza puzzled on it as she went back to work. Maybe it was just the attempt to salvage something of the weekend and his home that made him look so happy.

An hour later Liza was beginning to feel the effects of the hard work. She was hot for one thing, even in the chilly, depressing atmosphere of the flood-damaged house. Her legs and ankles ached with the effort of wading through the water with ill-fitting boots. She leaned wearily on the kitchen door-jamb as Robert waded towards her.

'You know, the water level is dropping dramatically. I wonder what the lane is like.'

'It might be passable,' Liza suggested, surprised she couldn't arouse more enthusiasm.

'I'll take a look.'

'I'll come with you.'

He took her hand and led her round the side of the house. 'Be careful here,' he warned. 'There are a couple of stone steps.'

Too late. She trod water and lurched forward. Robert caught her, and swung her round to stop her tumbling into the water. She was in his arms before she could catch her breath.

His arms locked around her and his mouth brushed her cheeks and sought her mouth with such ferocity that her senses spun. Negative thoughts were washed away in a storm of desire and need. She parted her lips willingly, matching his urgency. In her spinning mind she tried to latch on to the decision that needed to be made. To love him or not. What a hopeless choice. His tongue smoothed over the secret warmth of her mouth, urging her on to that decision. She clung to him, half-afraid of the power of the love that pulsed through her, half-afraid that he would pull back from her as he had done before.

Her fingers crazed through his hair, almost wanting to hurt him for the hold he had on her emotions. His hands slid over the front of her sweater and with a groan he drew away from her mouth and buried his head in her hair.

'I can't fight you any more, Liza; you understand what I'm saying?'

Her breath locked painfully in her throat and all she could do was nod against him. Slowly he pulled away from her, and put his hands each side of her face.

His eyes were darkly hooded with passion, a passion so unstoppable a refusal was out of the question. Refuse what her heart, her soul cried out for?

They stood gazing at each other, each fighting a losing battle within themselves. Nothing could be gained; Liza was resigned to that, but she didn't care. The longing for him outweighed the reasoning.

'You know what is going to happen, don't you?' He spoke softly as he smoothed the backs of his hands down her face.

Liza nodded, her eyes wide.

'Tell me honestly,' he breathed shakily, even now not sure. 'Is it what you want, Liza?'

She nodded again, her voice coming in a soft whisper. 'No strings...'

He shook his head vigorously, his eyes glazed with pain. 'Don't say that, Liza. It sounds so mercenary. I don't want it to be like that.'

She bit her lip, turned her face away and lowered her eyes to the water swirling around their feet. 'You're asking too much,' she whimpered. 'I have no control over myself any longer.'

He raised her chin. 'Believe me, it's no different for me,' he grazed.

She looked deeply into the darkness of his eyes and gave a small smile. 'Reluctant lovers,' she whispered emotionally.

He held her gaze in what seemed an eternity of time, and then slowly he echoed her words. 'Reluctant lovers.'

He took her hand and entwined his fingers in hers as if that small gesture was sealing the emotive words they had both uttered.

So, it was done. The decision made. Liza felt no pain, shut off that part of her soul that would later bleed for him. Now was what mattered, the future blanked off in her mind.

They turned back to the house, neither caring if the road out was passable or not.

Suddenly there was a shout from the driveway and they both turned, startled to see Jack wading towards them.

'Great news! Ed Blake has had an extension put on the exhaust of his Range Rover and is going around picking people up. I can arrange for him to take you out of here in about an hour,' Jack called.

Robert squeezed Liza's hand tightly. 'Too soon!' Robert shouted to him. 'We've still got unfinished business. Tomorrow would be fine, thanks, Jack.'

Jack stopped where he was, a wide grin spreading across his ruddy face. 'You're obviously coping all right.' He turned and started back along the drive.

'Yes, we're coping all right,' Robert muttered under his breath, giving Liza's hand another reassuring squeeze.

'What did he mean about the exhaust?' Liza asked as they stepped into only two inches of water in the kitchen.

'You can't start a car if the exhaust is underwater. Ed Blake, whoever he is, has obviously had some sort of periscope extension fitted to his car and is trying to rescue people who don't want to be rescued.'

Liza grinned. 'We could have got out of here in an hour,' she said.

He smiled back at her. 'It's the last thing we want, isn't it?'

She nodded, happy that he had made the decision for both of them.

Robert jammed close the kitchen door, and together they went through the house, shutting the windows and doors. As they worked, it seemed the awareness of each other heightened. The mundane job of securing the house up again didn't lessen their need. As the last window was sealed Robert swung her into his arms, his lips taking hers so urgently she gasped with sweet pleasure.

'You look and feel wonderful. I want to make love to you in those boots.'

'There's room enough for the two of us,' she laughed softly against his mouth.

He swept her up in his arms. 'Any more jokes like that and I'll make love to you ten times instead of seven!'

'Ten's my lucky number,' she murmured in his ear.

'So be it, lucky lady,' he said with a laugh as he bounded up the stairs with her clinging to him for dear life.

There was no more laughter as he lowered her to the bed; even when he removed their boots it was with slow sensuous movements. He lay beside her, smoothed her mass of frizz from her face and kissed her eyelids.

'You really are the most beautiful creature. I don't want this to end, Liza. I want it to go on and on,' he murmured softly.

She was afraid then, felt a sting of fear that wouldn't go away. His mouth grazed hers, gently at first and then deepening to a quickening need that didn't help allay those fears that crazed her. She wanted it to go on and on as well. A lifetime of loving him; but was it possible? As he eased his hand under her sweater and caressed her flesh she tensed, unwillingly, but a tightening of muscles nevertheless.

'Still unsure?' he murmured, lifting his head to look into her eyes.

Liza was surprised at the defence in his eyes, sure her assessment was correct. He was as afraid of this commitment as she was. She could stop it now; later would be too late. Now he was as vulnerable as she. She loved him for that, reached up and touched his mouth with her fingertips, willing him to go on. His teeth nipped at the soft flesh as he held her hand to his mouth.

'Don't be afraid. I'm glad it's still light. I want to see you, every part of you, explore every perfumed depth of you,' he murmured sensually.

Liza curled her arms around his neck and urged him down to kiss her lips, their urgency mounting so quickly Liza gasped at the onslaught of fevered *frisson* that tore through her.

He eased her sweater over her head, took her breasts in his lips and teased their peaks. Liza grazed her fingers across his hard-muscled back, pulling him against her. He rolled away to ease out of his clothes seconds, only seconds, before he was back with her, easing her thick socks from her feet and pulling down her tracksuit bottoms.

He smoothed his hand over her tiny silk briefs, but made no attempt to remove them. Liza moved restlessly, her skin pulsing with the need to feel his fingers caress her. She closed her eyes tightly in a spasm of frustration as he stroked the fine silk, finding the core of her femininity and caressing it through the material, heightening every pulse in her body till she could stand it no longer. Wildly tormented, she reached for him. He guided her hand and she grasped at him, her tremulous fingers wrapping around taut, silken flesh. She couldn't hold back. The effect of touching him so intimately and the rhythmic pulsing of his fingers on her was more than she could bear.

She cried out, cried his name as her climax rose furiously inside her, exploded like a shower of stars. 'Oh, God, I'm . . . I'm sorry.' The heat of his mouth shut her off. She clung to him, twisting and writhing with the deep heat that flamed inside her.

'Don't ever apologise for your sexuality,' he rasped against her mouth. 'It's beautiful, incredible.'

He moved her briefs away from her burning flesh, and touched her then, touched her so intimately she pulsed against him as if the last few frantic minutes had never happened. The need was stronger now, the need to feel him inside her.

She opened her tear-filled eyes, looked at him towering over her. She wanted to see his face as he entered her, wanted to see and feel and experience everything with him. His mouth parted in almost a snarl as he thrust into her, gently at first and then more strongly. That first ecstatic contact threw her into another spasm, her back arched and he smiled his triumph as she moved with him, gasping her joy.

Liza had never experienced such completeness. It was as if they had always meant to be, as if they had been born for each other. They moved heatedly together, almost fiercely in the frenetic need for each other. And then, with a cry of delighted shock, she came again, her muscles contracting so violently Robert cried out with her, his climax swelling and exploding inside her, spinning them out of control and into a world where only they and their passion existed.

The expected calm and tranquil winding-down never came.

'My turn to apologise,' Robert grated against her mouth. 'I lost control. I'll never get enough of you.' His mouth closed over hers and he started to move against her, gentle, firm thrusts that had her gasping her amazement. She was shocked at the power of his libido, shocked with herself for the response that was so immediate and so strong inside her. He aroused her instantly. This time they weren't so urgent, gave and took and shared their pleasure more deeply. Together they discovered and adored each other's bodies, sated their curiosity till their passion grew to such enormity that they were soon heading out of control again, exulting with cries of pleasure and passion.

Then came the peace and languid pleasure of satisfaction when Robert folded her into his arms and kissed the perspiration from her forehead. Exhausted, she lay in his arms, her heart gradually returning to near-normal. Her love for him was sealed for evermore, she realised sadly. He was a complete lover, perfect in every way, and how could life go on after this?

'What are you thinking?' he murmured.

'I was thinking what a good lover you are,' she murmured back.

'You're pretty perfect yourself.'

Liza squeezed her eyes tightly to stem the tears. That was the cold reality of it all. They were good together in bed. But she'd known the score before this had started, knew there were no guarantees, and yet she had wanted it to happen, maybe unconsciously had made it happen. She should have been stronger and more resolute in her determination to hold him off. But love had got in the way of good sense. She wondered what his excuse was.

Liza eased herself away from him. Got up and drew the curtains across the window. It was dark now. She lit the candles and stood shielding the flames till they took hold.

'Stay where you are,' Robert urged softly. 'I want to look at you naked by candlelight.'

She turned to him and smiled. How could she fight him when she loved him so much? Take this time together and enjoy, she vowed to herself.

'Tell me when I can get back into bed, and don't take too long. I could freeze out here,' she laughed.

'Poor darling,' he crooned. 'Come back this instant and let me warm you. Bring the champagne with you.'

'Champagne?' Her stomach tightened.

'It's in the box under the table, two champagne glasses as well.'

She spun back to the window, too angry and hurt to face him. With a groan Robert came to her, turned her into his arms. She rebelled, pounding her small fists on his chest. He held them tightly against him.

'I know exactly what you're thinking,' he grated roughly, 'but you are wrong, so very wrong.'

'Wrong to think you are a conniving rat? You brought that box up yesterday. What was your plan? To ply me with it and weaken me into submission?' She raised pained eyes to his. Her voice caught in her throat. 'But you didn't need it, did you? Because... because I came to you willingly, without wine to cloud my thinking. And now you want to celebrate your triumph...'

He forced her head against his chest, pressed his mouth to her flame hair. 'Don't, Liza; don't torture yourself and me; don't cheapen this precious thing we have.'

'Precious?' She raised her face and gazed into his eyes, so dark and softly glazed after their lovemaking.

'Yes, precious. Something very special between us. What has happened wasn't planned, by you or me. It was so inevitable that champagne never entered into it.'

She allowed him to lead her back to the bed, curl her into his arms under the duvet.

'Don't let's slip into questions and answers time, my darling. We can't predict what is going to happen tomorrow or the next day. I just want to share this time with you without even thinking beyond this night.'

Liza said nothing. Her love for him ached inside her. His feelings for her he'd made clear. Tonight was fine; tomorrow he'd face in the cold light of day. And what then? Would their affair continue, through their working days, into more nights like this?

She didn't know and, as his hands smoothed over her breasts, she didn't care. A small sliver of self-hate for her weakness played around her heart and then slid away as his tenderness overcame her. She went to him willingly, lovingly.

The next morning Ed Blake turned up early, taking Robert and Liza by surprise. They'd just finished breakfast, a joint culinary venture that had them in fits of laughter, comprising the last of the bacon and a tin of tomatoes Robert had opened and shot into the pan before realising they were peaches!

Ed Blake was the local garage-owner and village know-all, who promised Robert he'd get in touch with Mrs Harrison the housekeeper, and sort the house out before his next visit.

'Where do you want a lift to?' he asked, throwing their bags into the bag of the Range Rover.

'The nearest hotel that has hot water, electricity and a telephone,' Robert stated adamantly.

The drive out of the flooded area was a long one. Liza and Robert said nothing, but stared out of the window at the devastation all around them. Ed Blake was very forthcoming with disas-

ter stories, everyone in the area having a sorry
tale to tell.

Liza was depressed and cold by the time they
pulled up in front of the Challoner Hotel.

Robert thanked Ed for his help and tipped him
liberally before he left. Liza waved him off, glad
not to be hearing any more horror stories.

'I'll phone for Carl to drive down for us;
meanwhile, how does a hot shower grab you?'

'By the throat,' Liza laughed.

Robert booked a double room for a few hours
and as they waited impatiently for the receptionist to arrange it—apparently the hotel was almost
full to overflowing with flood victims—Robert
called Carl, who said he was on his way
immediately.

It was nearly lunchtime, and Robert ordered a
meal to be sent up to the room—roast beef and
all the trimmings.

'And a bottle of champagne on ice,' he added
with a laugh that was lost on the bewildered
receptionist.

Liza was first in the bathroom. 'A woman's
prerogative,' she giggled as she stripped.

'Male supremacy rules,' Robert retaliated,
outstripping her.

Together they flung themselves under the hot
shower, moaning and groaning and laughing with
the sheer ecstasy of it.

'Let me wash you,' Robert said hoarsely when
the laughter stopped. He lathered his hands and
ran them over her breasts, teasing circles of silky

foam over her flesh till she bit her lip with the sweet pleasure of it.

'I . . . I don't think we should . . .'

'I do,' he rasped, pressing his wet body to hers, leaving her in no doubt of the need that throbbed through him.

Their lovemaking in the shower was swift and impulsive, a fevered need that was undeterred by the awkwardness of the situation. Cold tiles pressed into Liza's back but her desire and insatiable longing for Robert dissolved her discomfort. They clung to each other after, letting the hot needles soothe their sated bodies. Then Robert shampooed her hair, rinsed it and gathered the mass of tendrils into a towel.

Later Liza sat at the dressing-table mirror and dried her hair with a blow-drier. Robert sat on the bed and made numerous phone calls—business calls.

Liza's euphoria began to fade. It was all coming to an end. Soon, very soon, the outside world would take over.

Their meal arrived and, though it looked delicious and they were both ravenous, they just picked at it.

Liza watched Robert's features. Already he was becoming Robert Buchanan the publishing tycoon again. Her lover no more.

They drank the champagne, Liza relishing every numbing mouthful of it. Somehow it helped ease the pain of loss.

Carl arrived to pick them up, and on the long drive back to London Robert told him what had happened. The rain, the flooding, the storm that had raged and the damage to the house. Liza listened, offering no comments of her own, and it was as if Robert were talking of something that had happened to someone else. She felt as if it had been a series of nightmares and dreams, and now she was awake and none of it had happened.

But it had; the ache deep inside her acknowledged that. The ache of his lovemaking and the pain of her love was testimony to the range of fevered emotions she had experienced this storm-ridden weekend.

At last they were home, Carl's car purring to a halt outside her town house. Robert got out with her.

'There's no need,' Liza told him quietly.

'There is,' was all he said as he carried her bag to the front door. He took the key from her hand and unlocked the door, pushed it open for her and followed her in.

She ran upstairs, flung her handbag down on the sofa and turned to him, not knowing what to say.

He lowered her overnight bag, crammed with wet ruined clothes, to the floor, and just stood looking at her. He didn't know what to say either, Liza realised with a heart-lurching jolt. He would want to let her down lightly, not to hurt her; he'd promised that. But he couldn't know how deeply she felt, how she now regretted every minute of her time with him. She hadn't prepared herself for that, the enormity of the pain. She had thought she would be able to override it somehow. Maybe she could if he chose his words carefully enough.

'Come here,' he said softly and like a lamb to the slaughter she went.

He framed her face in his hands, lowered his lips to her and kissed her. Not with passion as before, but a kiss she didn't understand.

He didn't say another word, just turned and left the room. She heard him shut the front door quietly behind him and her shoulders slumped with weariness.

He should have said something, preferably something that would have made her hate him. But a kiss like that...one she couldn't begin to comprehend...

The phone rang and she answered it, mechanically stating her number.

'Darling, I phoned your office and they said you weren't in. Are you all right? Not sick, I hope.'

Of course, it was Monday and she hadn't realised it. Back to the land of the living, Liza answered her mother in an unnaturally high voice. 'I'm fine, just taking a day off that was owed to me. How was Wales?'

She listened but didn't hear. Only after, when she had assured her mother all was well and put the phone down, did snippets of the conversation register. Yvonne and Graham were happy and well and sent their love and hoped to see her soon.

Liza was neither pleased nor displeased. All she felt was a dull ache in the pit of her stomach. Graham's rejection was nothing now, not even a sad memory. Robert filled her mind and her heart, and his inevitable rejection when it came would do more damage than a million Grahams of this world could inflict!

CHAPTER SEVEN

THERE was an unnatural silence as Liza walked into the office next morning. She was late, which was probably the reason for heads being turned in her direction. Unusual for her, but unavoidable, as her minicab, one of the perks of the job, had not turned up. A frantic phone call to the company had produced one on the double but nevertheless late.

She shut her office door, called out to Julia in the outer office, and slipped off her jacket.

'Oh, you're in,' Julia called back. 'I was beginning to get worried after yesterday.'

Liza suddenly realised she had no excuse prepared for her absence. She could hardly admit to the truth; that would set Magnum tongues wagging.

'My minicab didn't turn up on time,' was all she offered her assistant. As advertising-sales director she didn't need to answer to anyone on her whereabouts.

She leafed through correspondence from yesterday, pleased that Julia had responded so swiftly with replies, a pile of which awaited her signature. The phone rang and Liza lifted the receiver.

'Come to my office immediately and don't tell anyone where you are going.' The line went dead.

Robert had sounded very mysterious. She made her way to the lifts. Passing the telephone-sales consoles, she was sharply aware of an atmosphere, nothing specific, just a feeling that though they were all concentrating hard they were very aware of her presence.

She was even more aware of an atmosphere on Robert's floor. The secretaries at his reception unit looked away as she approached but David Cassals gave her his usual wide grin, and that put her mind at ease.

'All I can say is I'm very, very sorry, Liza,' were Robert's first grave words as she stepped into his plush office. He was seated at his desk, looking for all the world the publishing magnate. Not the loving man she had spent the weekend with.

Liza's heart slumped painfully. She had expected this, but so soon? She'd not given much thought to the professional side of their affair; the emotional side was going to be bad enough to cope with without losing the job as well. She'd been stupid and blind not to have anticipated this.

Bravely she raised her chin, her eyes clear and bright. 'When do you want me to leave?'

'Leave? I don't expect anything of the sort. I expect you to brazen it out as I'm going to do. I know it's easier for me, I'm used to it, but this has never happened to you before and——'

Liza's anger flared at his cool callousness. 'Short memory you have!' she interrupted bitterly. Had he forgotten Graham? 'You're not the first and no doubt you won't be the last. I'm getting well used to rejection. Probably the reason I was put on this earth——'

'Rejection? What the hell are you ranting on about?' He stood up, and came round the desk to her.

Liza backed away, wanting space and air between them. Her eyes widened fearfully as he reached out a hand for her. If he touched her she would cry, and that was the last thing she wanted him to witness—the breakdown of her emotions and laying open her true feelings for him.

'Liza,' he said softly, and then his hand came up to his forehead. 'You don't know, do you?'

Stupefied, Liza stared at him as he picked up a pile of newspapers from his desk, and handed them to her. He nodded to the leather sofa across the room. 'Sit over there and read them, Liza. I'll organise some coffee.' He went out of the room and hesitantly Liza stepped across the thick carpeting.

She sat down and unfolded the first. It was yesterday's paper, the headlines proclaiming the havoc the disastrous storms had dealt over the country. Why did Robert think she would be interested in that? She'd been among it all, seen it first hand... 'Oh, no!' she suddenly groaned, her eyes settling on the photograph at the bottom right of the front page.

Her head spun with a mixture of anger and sorrow. How could people do this? 'Even the mighty aren't immune!' the header screamed, and there was a picture of her and Robert leaning out of his bedroom window, she clutching at her wild hair and laughing.

She remembered that second helicopter, the one that had whirled her hair into a frenzy, the one that had had such a curious effect on Robert. For hours after it had circled the house he had appeared distracted. He'd known, known it was the Press!

The copy under the photo was all she could expect of such a newspaper, but oh, how it hurt when you were on the receiving end of it. She read it, re-read it till the tears of frustration welled hotly. There was more inside on the gossip page. More in other papers, today's as well. The whole world knew!

Furiously she leapt to her feet as Robert came back into the room with coffee.

'How could you?' she screamed. 'You knew, didn't you? Knew that helicopter was the Press?' She flung the papers across the room at him, covered her face with her hands and burst into tears.

Robert put the coffee down on the coffee-table and tried to gather her into his arms, but she flung him aside and went to lurch from the room. He grabbed her then, fiercely pulled her back and held her at arm's length.

'You're going nowhere in that state. Do you want to make it worse for us?'

'For us?' she blazed. 'What have you got to lose? According to the papers I'm just the latest of a long line of redheaded mistresses! Great for your macho image but what about me?'

His eyes were dark and unfathomable as he gazed down at her face. 'I've said I'm sorry——'

'Sorry? Sorry?' Her lips tightened to a thin line of fury. 'It's not enough, Robert, not nearly enough. How can I face Magnum? It's already started—the strange looks, the staff avoiding my eyes.' Now she knew the reason for the strained atmosphere. 'How can I command respect from my staff when they all know I'm bedding the boss?'

'No one knows that!' Robert protested. 'It's only speculation——'

'It's enough!' Liza flung back at him. 'You should know that more than anyone else in the world! Look at that photo, the two of us hanging out of your bedroom window. We might as well have been snapped in the bed. It's all the same!'

She slumped down on the sofa and covered her face again. It was all so unbelievable; yet another nightmare to torture her waking hours.

'I'll sue them!' she breathed at last. 'I'll damn well sue them! It's libel, isn't it?' she asked Robert plaintively.

'Afraid not,' he told her mournfully. He sat down next to her and handed her a cup of coffee.

'Do you want a shot of brandy in that? You've had a nasty shock.'

Was that all he could offer, something to numb the shock? 'Yes,' she answered defiantly, thrusting the cup at him. 'Fill it to the brim. I'm going to be a raging alcoholic by the time this is all over, *if* it's ever over!'

Robert added a dash of brandy to the cup and handed it back to her. 'Drink isn't the answer,' he murmured.

'What is the answer, then? And why can't I sue these creeps? It's defamation of character, isn't it?'

'Hardly. The freedom of the Press and all that. They're entitled to print what they have. We were snapped at my bedroom window, isolated and trapped by the floods.'

'No reason to suppose we are having an affair,' she retorted.

'Truth is, we are,' Robert stated flatly.

Liza bit her lip. It sounded awful. An affair, a sordid affair. 'We could deny it,' she blurted.

'That would be a lie.'

'Yes, but only you and I know it!'

Robert started to pace the floor. She wondered why he was looking so sick about the whole business. He'd lost his honourable reputation years ago—that was if he'd ever had one!

'You forget the hotel we booked into for a couple of hours.'

'Rubbish! People book into hotels for all manner of reasons,' she protested hotly. 'The people who were there were flood victims, not having affairs!'

'Will you stop this?' Robert suddenly grated furiously. 'It's happened, Liza. You're only winding yourself up unnecessarily by thrashing through it this way.'

'Yes, because I'm the injured party in all this. It's nothing to you. As you said, you're well used to it. I'm not. I'm hurt and angry and, worse, I'm ashamed, terribly, terribly ashamed...'

'Don't be ashamed——'

'Don't be ashamed!' she echoed scornfully. 'How can you possibly know how I feel?' Her hand flew to her mouth. 'Oh, God! My parents! What will my poor parents think? Their daughter's face, plastered over the pages of those...those disgusting papers!'

'Don't tell me they read pulp like this?' Robert offered ineffectually.

'They don't!' Liza protested hotly. 'But neighbours and shopkeepers might, and that's worse. Hearing it from some grinning, leering greengrocer. Here's your sprouts, Mrs Kay; fancy your Liza carrying on like that...'

Robert was across the room and hauling her out of the sofa before she could finish. He held her by the shoulders and shook her angrily.

'Will you stop this? It doesn't help, Liza. You're only torturing yourself.' He loosened his fierce grip on her, almost caressed her shoulders. 'How do you think I feel about all this?' he asked softly, rhetorically. 'It's hurting me too, tearing me apart inside to think of what you're going through.'

Her face crumbled. Her strength drained from her. Shaking her head miserably, she croaked, 'You knew, Robert. You knew that helicopter was the Press. You lied to me, said they were sightseers.'

He pulled her hard against him, pressed her head into his shoulder. 'I didn't lie intentionally. I suspected they were the media but I didn't want to alarm you. You'd been through enough already without that hassle. I honestly didn't know they had taken a photo——'

'You thought they might, though. That's why you hauled me back inside the house. Very honourable. Pity your sense of gallantry didn't carry you through the rest of the weekend!' she ground out sarcastically.

A sigh of resignation rattled in his chest. Liza felt it, felt the slow beat of his heart against her breasts.

'Yes, you're right,' he admitted slowly. 'My conduct was inexcusable. All I can offer is my sincerest apologies.'

There was nothing more for him to offer, Liza reasoned hopelessly. Nothing more he *wanted* to offer! She brought her hands up and eased him away from her.

'I'll have to leave, Robert. I can't face the staff, can't face them tittering behind my back...' It was unbearable, the thought that everyone knew.

'There's no need for that.' His hand came up and tilted her chin. 'There's a solution to all this,' he said seriously, his eyes searching hers as if looking for an answer in their hurt green depths. 'We can put the rumours and speculation to rest once and for all. Marry me, Liza.'

Shock waves spiralled crazily down her spine. She opened her mouth to speak but nothing happened. A phone rang in the distance, as far away as if it were in another world. Robert's eyes blackened furiously and then he released her, turned to the phone and grabbed at it ferociously.

'I thought I told you to hold my calls...I don't care how insistent she is...tell her to go to hell!' He slammed down the phone and turned back to Liza, his eyes once again searching hers.

Liza's head hadn't stopped spinning in those brief incredulous seconds as Robert had taken the call. Now nausea added to her agony. No prizes for guessing who that was calling. Lady Victoria. In spite of her own misery and shame she could feel sorry for the poor woman. It must have shaken her to read of Robert's latest conquest when she had such high hopes for their future together. They were all victims, every damned woman he'd ever encouraged to fall in love with him.

'What's your answer, Liza?'

'This!' She raised her hand and slapped him hard across the face, wishing she'd had the strength to ball her fist to add power to the blow.

He rubbed his chin ruefully. 'I half expected that from you,' he said breathlessly.

'Well, here's something that will take the other half of your breath away.' Her decision was an instant, reckless one, born out of anger, bitterness and a sudden spurt of pride. She'd been weak but wasn't any more. Damn the lot of them! 'I'm not resigning after all,' she told him firmly. 'You can try sacking me if you wish, but I'll take you to the unfair dismissal tribunal. See how that sort of publicity affects the sales of your precious magazines!'

He glowered furiously at her. 'I have no intention of firing you, but don't use threats like that again, Liza.'

'And don't ever insult me with a proposal of marriage like that again!' she stormed.

She went to the door, amazed at her new-found strength. She was going to cope if it killed her!

In the lift down to the sales floor she flicked at her hair and rubbed viciously under her eyes to smear away the last vestige of a tear. She pulled down her suit jacket and smoothed her narrow skirt over her bottom. She was going to brave this out. The rumours would stop in time, especially if there was no reason for them to go on. She'd keep her distance from Robert from now on. And he'd do likewise if he had any sense.

She strode purposefully out of the lift across to one of the telephone-sales girls, even managing to swing her hips defiantly as she went. She sensed all eyes were on her. Let them look and speculate and eat their hearts out. She didn't care what they thought!

'What have you got so far this morning, Corinne?'

'Two back pages, four half-pages and a four-page promotion for Sensual Perfumes,' Corinne told her proudly.

'Great,' Liza enthused with a wide grin. 'Keep on fizzing.' With that she turned and walked into her office, and shut the door quietly behind her.

The temptation to collapse into floods of renewed tears was enormous, but Liza steeled herself. Though Julia seemed to be keeping her distance, rattling and bleeping away at her computer in the other office, Liza didn't dare to give in and show any signs of emotion. She sat at her desk and breathed deeply for a few seconds. Then she reached for the phone and tapped out her parents' code. She hoped she had the strength to offer some sort of explanation to her mother!

Robert came into Liza's office when Julia had gone to lunch with Nigel and the rest of the sales team. There was no one around, and that annoyed Liza.

'Is this how it's going to be, you sneaking in here when you're sure no one is around?' she asked bitterly.

He leaned back against the window-sill. 'Not at all. As you rightly said, I have nothing to lose and you can obviously handle the situation.' He folded his arms across his chest and studied her.

'It's not going to be easy, you know. We have to work together. Everything will be misinterpreted from now on: sales meetings, board meetings—every time we are together the staff will gossip.'

'You want me to go, don't you?' Her bravado wavered slightly. It was going to take some strength of character to weather this out. She took a deep breath. She could do it. Surprisingly her mother had been very supportive, giving her a little more courage to fight with.

'I don't want you to go,' he said quietly. 'You are more than excellent at your job.'

She gave him a cynical smile. 'Of course, we mustn't forget Magnum.' She levelled her green eyes at him. 'You know, my mother was brilliant when I called her. She put everything into perspective for me. She didn't want to know what had happened down there at your house, said the world was full of silly people, and the people that mattered were the ones who stood by me. So far only my parents have offered such support——'

'Mine doesn't count, then?'

Liza's eyes narrowed. 'Was that crazy proposal of marriage your support? I wouldn't marry you if we were the last two people on earth and were responsible for procreating a new world!'

He said nothing for a long while, a long while in which she suspected she might have hurt him with that remark. But he had a skin as tough as a rhino, she convinced herself—insult-proof!

'So our time together meant nothing to you?' he eventually said, raising his eyes from the carpet he had been studying so intently.

'About as much as it meant to you!' she snapped back cruelly. The ice was back, her heart frosted over as if his sun had never shone on it.

'How the hell would you know how I feel?' His words came out with such bitterness she jerked her head to meet his eyes, but saw nothing but jet hardness. She looked away, lowered her eyes to her desk.

'I think you feel the same way that I do,' she forced out. 'It was nice while it lasted, a pleasant way to while away the hours——'

'You hard...' He stopped, lowering his hands to his side in defeat.

Bitch! That was what he'd been about to say. Even though he hadn't she felt the stab of it in the pit of her stomach. If only he knew the torture she was going through. The gossip hurt, but loving him was a worse ordeal to have to live through. Her mouth thrust out such harsh words but her heart died a little each time.

Robert took a deep breath, a resolute breath. 'We're leaving for Amsterdam on Thursday, and we'll be back Friday night. Madrid can wait till things have quietened down. Be prepared for the worst,' he told her.

And what was that supposed to mean? She doubted if it was what she was thinking: that she would be living in his pocket again, sharing the same hotel, wanting him more than ever. The awful truth was that, even though he had hurt her, exposed her to the worst of publicity, she still cared. She didn't want to, hated her weakness, but love couldn't be swept aside so easily.

'The Press, you mean,' she murmured without looking at him.

'What else? I won't subject myself to another weekend like the one we've just been through.' Liza had no space to puzzle what he meant by that before he went on. 'If you can possibly tear your thoughts away from the injustices of life that have swamped you this morning give a thought to how all this happened...'

She raised her eyes to him. His brow was creased; a muscle pulsed at his jawline.

'I've never been troubled by the Press at my home before,' he went on. 'In a way I've almost respected them for that small discretion. But it appears that someone must have tipped them off that we were down there this weekend.'

'You don't think I——?' she started to protest, her colour rising at the thought.

'No, I don't, and spare me the blushes of indignation. You're a lot of things, Liza, but, from what little I know of you, I wouldn't put you down as a heartless opportunist.' Her heart raced furiously at that. 'But someone did. The Press don't hire helicopters for nothing.'

'But they do when a flood devastates half a county...'

'Gossip columnists don't,' he insisted darkly. 'That helicopter came over for the express purpose of snapping a potential scandal.'

The colour drained from Liza's cheeks at the thought that someone must have planted the seed of the story.

'What about your staff, your secretaries?' she suggested, aghast at the thought of such disloyalty.

'My personal staff I trust completely, and, besides, none of them knew where I was last weekend.'

'Are you implying it was someone here?' She flung her hands in the air to encompass her office. She stood up shakily. 'I realise you are trying to pass the buck, but that's ridiculous! No one from here knew where I was going either—even I didn't till the last moment!' A new, disturbing thought pulsed through her, one she kept to herself. 'So how does that affect this trip of ours to Amsterdam? We can't keep that under wraps.'

'That's what I meant by being prepared. I have a feeling the Press won't let up. We'll have an escort for sure; more than likely be hounded by the continental Press as well. They are even worse at raking scandal than the UK——'

'I won't go!' Liza snapped, turning her back on him like a petulant child.

'You will,' Robert insisted. 'You'll face it. Where's all that fight you've thrown in my face this morning?'

'It's fast disintegrating,' she murmured. Slowly she turned to face him. 'Robert, it will stop, won't it?' She raked her hair from her face, her eyes wide and appealing to him. 'Because if it doesn't,' she whispered, 'I'm not going to be able to cope.'

She felt defeat facing her. She was trying so hard to be strong, but every time he opened his mouth he was making it sound blacker. Now he suspected some sort of company treachery, and how could you work knowing someone was pointing a knife at your heart all the time? And Amsterdam—it was going to be the test of all time on her emotions.

He stepped towards her and she lifted her open palms to stop him. She knew he was going to attempt to console her, knew it with a thud of her heart.

'I'll be all right,' she told him, drawing a deep breath. 'Let's try to put this behind us, try not to think about it.' She tilted her chin. 'What time will we be leaving Thursday?'

'I'll have my secretary type out a schedule for you. Bring something dressy to wear for Thursday evening. There's a nice restaurant by the River Amstel I'd like to take you to,' he said softly as he turned to the door.

Liza closed her eyes in sufference and snapped them open as he turned the doorknob. How could he even think of such a thing?

'Robert, is that wise?' she uttered helplessly.

He looked at her, feigning puzzlement for a second. 'The restaurant?' Then he smiled. 'Not wise at all, but neither of us are very clever where our emotions are concerned, are we?'

'I...I meant...the...media,' she stammered.

'I know exactly what you meant.' He closed the door after him.

For a long, long time Liza stared at the door. It was going to be intolerable, unbearable, and she didn't have to suffer it. She could get up and walk out of his and Magnum's life this very minute, but that would take more strength than staying. It wasn't the job that was holding her back, it was him. The love for him that was draining her life-blood away, leaving her weak and indecisive. She could have accepted his proposal, married him in the hope he might learn to love her; after all, he must care enough to be prepared to marry her to stop the gossip. But it wasn't enough. It would be a marriage of convenience, *her* convenience; he wouldn't give up his freedom and Lady Victoria and whatever other women he had in his life.

She tried to concentrate on her work, tried hard to stem the feeling of desolation that burned the backs of her eyes. She looked up when Julia came back from lunch. Suddenly the unease that Robert had stirred in her flooded back. Could Julia have been the one to inform the Press of her movements last weekend? She'd known she was going to work with Robert—hadn't she bandied around a few suggestive remarks about being cooped up with the delicious Buchanan all weekend? But no; she had thought they were working from the office. Liza's forehead broke out into a sweat: she could have overheard, though, when Robert had calmly informed her they were going to work from his home; she'd been in her office at the time, Liza remembered.

The busy afternoon vanquished the thoughts from her mind, but they involuntarily eased back when she was on her way home after work.

Julia had not spoken about the newspaper reports and that was unusual for her normally outspoken assistant; mind you, no one else had mentioned it either, no doubt too afraid of the wrath of Robert Buchanan. But Julia was close to her and it was out of character for her not to have made some cheery, or otherwise, reference to it. Guilty conscience, maybe. But why should her assistant do such a heartless thing? She'd always thought they had a good working relationship. The girl couldn't be jealous of her and Robert, a possible motive but one she dismissed because of Julia's love for Nigel. If she'd sacked Nigel, as Robert had suggested, that could have been another motive, but she hadn't; she'd given him a second chance.

No, it couldn't be Julia; she had no idea where Robert lived anyway. But... the media had their sources and no doubt could find out anything if fed enough information to fire a story...

Liza thanked the minicab driver and got out of the car. This was ridiculous. She was beginning to think as unscrupulously as the media acted. Yes, she was getting paranoid, she decided as she looked to left and right for reporters concealing themselves behind shrubs in the small landscaped courtyard. No one around. That was the best thing that hadn't happened all day!

CHAPTER EIGHT

BY THE time Thursday morning came Liza was convinced her first suspicions were right and Julia was the informer. It was what Julia *wasn't* saying that confirmed it for Liza. Surprisingly, yesterday had been perfectly normal. No sly looks in the office. But Julia's silence was far from normal. Not one cheeky remark about her and the delicious Buchanan.

It wasn't in Liza's character to dwell too deeply on such suspicion, but something like this had never happened in her life before and besides, while she was puzzling it through her mind, it set a precedence over thoughts of Robert.

'What time are you leaving for the airport?' Julia asked when Liza walked into the office that morning with her overnight bag.

Immediately Liza tensed. With an inner warning to herself she let go and relaxed. This suspicion was silly. Julia was entitled to know her schedule, and it was no secret anyway—too many people were involved in getting the trip together.

She passed her the sheet of paper which Robert's secretary had prepared for her. Flight times, hotel booking, times of meetings with the Amsterdam Magnum team. It was a tight schedule, every minute of their time spoken for, except for this evening. After eight o'clock cocktails at the hotel—with Johann Klein, the managing director of the overseas corporation—there was a yawning gap till nine the next morning!

'I needn't have come in this morning, but I wanted to make sure I hadn't overlooked anything yesterday. You won't forget to phone Carson Studios, will you?'

Julia grinned. 'You've reminded me umpteen times already. Not like you at all. You know I can hold the fort for a couple of days.'

Liza gave her a reluctant smile. Was her stress showing? She'd tried so hard to carry on as if nothing had happened. Robert had barely shown his face in the Magnum offices since Tuesday, and that had helped.

The phone rang and Julia, standing by Liza's desk, lifted it and handed it to Liza. 'Mr Buchanan.' Liza took it and Julia mouthed she was going to get a coffee and did Liza want one? Liza nodded her reply and gave her attention to Robert.

'I've a business call to make before we leave, Liza. Take a taxi to the airport and I'll meet you there. OK?'

'Fine.'

He clicked off, and before Liza had time to reflect on the arrangement the phone rang again.

'Liza?'

It took a couple of seconds before her brain registered and recognised the voice. 'Graham?' she breathed incredulously.

'How are you, Liza? We've been worried sick about you. All that terrible business in the papers.'

Liza could actually smile. 'I'm fine, Graham. It was nothing...'

'Nothing? Yvonne is distraught for you. She wanted to come down to see you but she's plagued with sickness at the moment.'

'Oh, dear; it's normal though, isn't it? Congratulations, by the way.'

'Thanks.' She could see the grin on his face. 'We're delighted. What I rang for was to say I'm coming down to town for a few days to see my agent. I've another book finished and he's pretty excited with it. I'd like to come and see you. Your mother said you're coping with all this business, but I wanted to give you some more family support.'

'I'm off to Amsterdam in a couple of hours.' She hesitated only fleetingly. 'I'm back Friday afternoon, though. Why don't you drop round in the evening?'

The door clicked open and Julia came in with two coffees.

'Marvellous,' Graham enthused. 'It's been a long time, Liza. It will be nice to have some time together. I think we need to get this rift between us sorted out now that the baby is coming.'

'Yes, you're right,' Liza breathed on a smile. 'Friday night after this business trip will be a welcome respite. I'll cook a meal for the two of us.'

'That will be super. See you Friday, then. Bye.'

Liza put down the receiver with a happy smile. Some good had come out of this mess. The family was closing ranks. Graham was family now, her brother-in-law, not even her old love. In a way Robert had made it all clear to her. Her love for him surpassed all, fading any misconceptions of the feeling she thought she still had for Graham into insignificance. Now she could face Graham without any bitterness. It was a pleasant thought.

Her face was beaming as she said to Julia, 'Book me a taxi to the airport, Julia. Robert is meeting me at the airport.'

She sipped her coffee and stretched back in the chair. If she could only dispel Robert Buchanan from her life she might have a chance for her future, though at the moment it all looked ominously bleak. Her depression hung like a cloud over her waking hours, her love for him filled every aching second of her thoughts. One step at a time, though. Graham's response had momentarily cheered her. Maybe with the support of her family she could try and forget.

'Oh, no!' Liza cried in dismay, shielding her face from the predatory cameras with her briefcase in the airport terminal.

Robert took her firmly by the arm and they stepped up their stride.

'That's enough, fellas,' he directed firmly yet good-heartedly to a group of jostling photographers.

'Business or pleasure in Amsterdam, Miss Kay?' someone called out.

Liza was about to open her mouth to call back a suitable retort to that when Robert increased the pressure on her arm till the pain swept speech from her lips.

'I don't understand why you let them get away with it,' Liza protested as they buckled up in the business-class section of their KLM flight to Schiphol airport. 'You were almost polite to them.'

'If you show anger it makes it worse. They love it. Besides, they are only doing their job.'

'You sound as if you're on their side.'

Robert shrugged. 'I don't mind the publicity. It sells my magazines. Keeps me in the public eye, and in this business it isn't a bad thing.'

'My feelings don't count,' she said scornfully.

'They do, and if the pressure hots up and it becomes unbearable for you I'll put a stop to it.'

'You think you have the power to do that?' she half laughed. 'Mr Big in magazine publishing you might be, but the tabloids are something else!'

'I like to think I have friends among them,' he stated quietly. 'And if they don't pull out all the stops when I ask I'll just have to buy them out, won't I?'

Liza pulled out the flight magazine from the rack in front of her and flicked through it, seeing nothing. 'That's your answer to everything. If it doesn't jump when you whistle, buy it out!'

'One take-over bid failed miserably, though, didn't it?'

'Which one was that?' she said with little interest, found an article that might hold her enthralled for five minutes and bent her red head over it.

'Liza Kay Enterprises turned down my offer.'

The magazine slid out of her fingers to the floor. She turned to face him, annoyed to see he was stretched back in his seat, his eyes closed.

'Are you surprised? It was a silly offer, one not worth considering!'

'*I* considered it very thoroughly. Marriage is a very serious business,' he murmured without opening his eyes. 'But don't think I'm going to let up on you, Liza Kay Enterprises. I haven't failed in a take-over yet.'

Face flushed with indignation, Liza bent down to retrieve her magazine. Robert's hand came down and softly caressed the back of her head. A caress so positive and frightening that she wasn't aware of the sudden thrust of the engines as they took off. She flung herself back in her seat, swallowed hard, and stared determinedly out of the window. He felt sorry for her but he wasn't going to win, wasn't going to take her over as if she were some poor, ailing magazine that needed rescuing from the slush pile!

*   *   *

Liza only had time to unpack in the lovely Hotel Delft before Robert knocked on her bedroom door and whisked her away to the Magnum offices in a staff car with chauffeur.

The hotel had surprised her, being a last-minute change of the scheduled plan, engineered by Robert in case someone at Magnum had informed the Press of their intended whereabouts. The Delft wasn't one of the main Amsterdam hotel blocks that one saw in every city of the world, but a quiet back-street building, tall and narrow with no frontage but a pretty cobbled street edged with ornate balustrade and a small canal flowing beyond. Spring had come early to the lovely old city, and blossom hung heavy from the trees in the street.

What little Liza saw of the interior of the hotel was exquisite—Dutch antiques, including a superb marquetry cabinet in the foyer. There were few rooms, which indicated the exclusiveness of the hotel. Robert's room was next to hers, on the first floor with a view over the canal and a flower barge moored directly outside.

Liza took to the city immediately, loved the bustle and the trams and the hordes of cyclists, some with passengers perched side-saddle on panniers at the back, precariously weaving in and out of the traffic. The sights and smells of a foreign country numbed her senses to Robert for a while, and she was grateful for that.

Magnum offices, Amsterdam were much the same as the Knightsbridge outfit but smaller. The staff she had liaised with over the phone were as eager to meet her as she was them. Introductions were made and Robert left her in the advertising department while he joined Johann Klein in the boardroom.

Though she was fully occupied and absorbed, she still found herself taking unwillingly tentative glances at the door for Robert's return. When he did come back their eyes locked in a fleeting exchange, Liza the first to break it in a wave of shyness tinged with anger. Looks like that she could live without.

Too soon it was over, and Robert was at her side to whisk her back to the hotel. Meetings were arranged for the following morning.

'What did you think?' Robert asked, stretching his long legs in the back of the limousine.

'Marvellous. To be honest I'd imagined the set-up to be different, but they work on much the same lines as we do in the UK.'

'Yes, we're all Europeans now, not Dutch or British or French.'

'Shame really,' Liza mused, 'though unity isn't a bad thing, I suppose, so long as we all hang on to something of our individuality. Their advertising is slightly different, though—an awful lot of naked bodies!' she laughed.

He laughed with her and it was only when they reached the hotel she realised his hand had been over hers in the back of the car. She could still feel its warmth when she unlocked her bedroom door.

'I'll give you a shout in an hour,' he said as he opened his door.

'An hour?' Liza frowned at her watch. 'I thought we were having drinks with Klein at eight.' It was only six now.

'I cancelled it,' he told her lightly. 'And I want to leave for the restaurant earlier than planned. So far we've been lucky with the Press but I want no interruptions tonight. It's going to be our time, not theirs.' He went into his room and shut the door.

Liza showered and got ready for dinner with trepidation in her heart. What a complex man he was. She never knew which way he would swing. Had he been serious about not letting up on her? Or was it another of his throw-away remarks, sure to wind her up again? And 'our time'; so personally said, as if it meant something to him.

She stood in front of the mirror when she was ready, and smoothed down her dress. It was jade silk, sleek and clingy with a matching shawl that she scooped casually around her shoulders. Her hair was loose; flame-gold and red, it cascaded around her face and across the shawl in tiny spirals of curl. He'd said she had a Renaissance beauty... Liza closed her eyes. It seemed everything he had ever said to her spun in her mind at that moment. If only he hadn't offered to marry her to save her face she might believe that they had some chance together.

There was a light tap on her door and Liza opened her eyes, her heart racing. How was she going to get through this evening, loving him and hurting so much inside? She read the pain in her own eyes in the mirror. Heaven forbid he should see it. She gathered up her tiny gold evening-bag and went to the door.

'Beautiful,' he breathed, and took her hand and led her to the lift.

The night air was cool but not unpleasant. Robert, in a black evening suit, led her across the narrow cobbled street to the flower barge.

'Robert, look at those baskets of fuchsias,' she enthused. The barge was decked with them; they hung everywhere from iron hooks, a poignant reminder of Robert's lovely conservatory. There were tubs of tulips, daffodils, carnations of every imaginable colour, even blue.

'They're dyed,' Robert told her with a laugh as she exclaimed she'd never seen blue carnations before. 'These are the real thing, though.' He scooped a huge bundle of pale yellow roses from a tub and thrust them in her arms. Liza buried her face in their heady sweetness and wanted time to stand still. When she raised her eyes Robert was paying for them, laughing with the enormous Dutch lady in her colourful embroidered apron.

Liza waited for him, tears nearly spilling from her eyes. She didn't want this—the flowers, his being so nice to her.

'Why did you do that?' she murmured, her voice so tremulous she thought it would break.

He took her arm and guided her to a small jetty the other side of the flower barge. 'Later. I'll tell you later,' he said softly.

'What are you doing?' she suddenly exclaimed as a motor boat drew up alongside and Robert stepped into it, holding out his hand to her. She stepped gingerly down into the boat. 'It's the only way to get to this particular restaurant and, besides, it's romantic, don't you think?'

Liza's nerves stretched over the pain barrier. This was so unfair. To him it was a whim, a pleasant way to pass an evening in Amsterdam. To her it was almost beyond endurance. She sat next to him on luxurious leather seating at the back of the boat, clutching the thornless roses on her lap. She couldn't speak for the tightness of her throat and it was pointless to try: the roar of the powerful engine drowned out any attempt to converse. Her mind said it all, soundlessly. Told him what her lips couldn't. That she hated him for this.

White lights were strung along the canal-side like luminous strings of pearls. Tiny bridges looped prettily over the water, their lights reflected in the canal. Liza ached to enjoy it but her heart was so torn that pleasure was out of the question.

The driver steered the boat out of the narrow canal into the rougher waters of the river and Liza tightened her shawl around her shoulders as the wind caught her hair and flurried it around her face. Robert looped his arm around her and drew her closer to him. She didn't fight it, but bit her lip and endured it.

Mercifully, this part of the journey was soon over and the boat drew into a jetty with a flurry of spray. The restaurant was a converted canal barge hauled up on to the banks of the river. The conversion was superb. If you closed your eyes to the surroundings you could have been in an exclusive bistro in the heart of Paris.

'Do you like it?' Robert asked as they sat by a window that overlooked the river and the brightly lit tourist barges that chugged slowly along.

Liza lay the roses on the seat next to her. 'It's lovely, the flowers too.' She took a deep breath and raised her eyes to look at him. 'You didn't have to do all this, Robert. I know why, and it's sweet and kind of you, but not necessary.'

He smiled. 'If I knew what you were talking about I might be able to offer something back.'

With a sigh Liza clasped her hands tightly in her lap and shook her head. 'Don't make it difficult for me. You know exactly what I mean. You're embarrassing me, do you know that?'

His eyes softened. 'I didn't mean to embarrass you. If you think tonight is some sort of consolation prize for what has happened this week, I'm sorry. It's not meant to be.'

'So what is it?'

He shrugged lightly, as if the question was beyond him. His answer, softly spoken, clearly stated that it was. 'I'm not sure, not sure of very much these days.'

The waiter hovered and Liza didn't press it. She glanced around as Robert ordered drinks. There were few other diners, probably the inaccessibility of the place bringing out only the determined diners. She asked Robert to order for her.

'I'm not very familiar with Dutch cuisine,' she added with a smile.

'It doesn't matter here. It's *nouvelle cuisine* and that's more or less the same the world over.' He turned to the waiter and ordered in Dutch for the two of them.

'I didn't know you could speak the language,' she said, surprised and reluctantly impressed.

'I don't,' he grinned. 'Menus only, and of course a polite please and thank you. It gets me by.' He leaned back in his seat and looked at her. 'So far, so good. No Press. Hopefully a coup somewhere in the world has distracted them.'

Liza let her tension drain from her. Maybe that was why she was feeling so stressed; apart from her feelings for him, she realised that the thought of being followed by photographers had been slowly building up inside her, making her tense and wary.

'I hope it's all over now,' she sighed. 'I'd hate to be a pop star. They must never have a life of their own.'

'Something you have to expect if you're in the public eye.'

She didn't know whether to broach the subject of Lady Victoria but decided it needed to be said. And now that the hysteria was dying down she wanted him to know how sorry she was.

'You...you and Lady Victoria...' she started, hesitating because of the sudden clouding of his eyes. She bit her lip. He *did* care for her. She wondered what he must have said to her to re-assure her. 'I'm truly sorry for what happened. I...mean...it must have been awful for her to see...see us in the papers and read all that dreadful gossip.'

His eyes cleared and for a second he looked at her in disbelief.

'I'm...I'm sorry...' she lowered her lashes '...I shouldn't have brought it up.' She reached for her wine glass. Robert's hand closed over hers before she could reach it.

'Sometimes you amaze me,' he said throatily. 'I can't believe you think I care what she thinks or feels.'

Liza's heart steeled. He really was a hard and uncaring man where women were concerned.

'Vicky and I know the score with each other. To quote a much hackneyed cliché, we are just good friends. I thought I made that clear to you.'

She looked at him numbly. 'Yes, but she cares for you. She phoned you when I was in your office...you told her to go to hell...'

'I told Phillipa Statton, editor of *Fine Homes* magazine, to go to hell. She's pestering me for editorship on one of our mags. I don't want her, have told her on numerous occasions, but she won't take no for an answer.' His eyes blazed angrily for a second and then they softened. 'You see how easily people can jump to the wrong conclusion from an overheard phone call...?'

'I'm sorry,' Liza murmured, drawing her hand away from his. 'I just thought——'

'You thought wrongly. You think wrongly about a lot of things, Liza. You thought my marriage proposal was uttered out of sympathy.'

Her eyes widened angrily. 'It was! You more or less said it would curb the gossip.'

'I suppose it must have sounded that way,' he conceded, 'but I've never proposed before——'

'And if you do it that way again you'll never get accepted,' she blurted, not thinking what she was saying. 'Women want hearts and flowers, not...' She stopped, appalled at the thought he might think she wanted him to ask her again.

Robert smiled, a strange secretive smile of knowing. 'Well, darling,' he drawled, 'you have the flowers and I suppose you have my heart. What more do you want?'

Her colour rose. 'I...I...didn't...mean...' She didn't finish, but froze as the waiter placed tiny scampi bathed in champagne sauce in front of her. He moved away and she gulped a breath, staring at her plate, not daring to raise her eyes to his. 'I...I didn't mean it to sound the way it did. I meant the next time you propose to another woman, not...not me.'

'But you're the woman I want to marry,' he breathed so softly she barely heard.

She let her fork rest at the side of her plate, bravely raised wide green eyes to his. 'Don't, Robert,' she uttered weakly, every pulse in her throbbing with pain. 'You once said you wouldn't hurt me, but you are.'

'And if you're hurt that means I'm not making a fool of myself. You care for me as much as I care for you.'

She looked away, not able to hold his gaze. 'I ... I don't understand you.'

'You do,' he insisted quietly. 'And I understand you. The trouble is neither of us can say it, admit that we love each other.'

There were no words; she fought to find them, to urge them to her lips.

'Why don't you say it, Liza? I'll help you. I don't believe either of us could have experienced last weekend, the closeness, the lovemaking, the intimacy of that terrible weekend, without a great deal of feeling for each other.'

'It was because of the awfulness of it that we did what we did!' she protested, her voice broken and cracked with emotion. She pushed her plate away. She couldn't eat. 'Don't mistake that for love,' she whispered. 'Put any two people in the same situation and it would be inevitable.'

His eyes darkened and he gazed at her, a frown creasing his brow. 'Are you telling me I am making a fool of myself and you felt nothing?'

She said nothing, just wanted to be away from here, back at the hotel where she could shut the door and let the emotion drain out of her. How could she tell him she loved him, wanted him beside her every living breathing hour of her life?

'I can't and won't believe that you don't feel the way I do...'

'And what is *that way*?' she breathed.

He let out a ragged sigh. 'From the moment I first set eyes on you, I wanted you. Yes, you're right. Wanted you. Not love, not love that I recognised, that is, but on reflection it couldn't have been anything else. I'm obsessed with you, Liza. If that's love, I admit it. Not having been in that condition before it took a long time for it to sink in. I asked you to marry me because I want you in my life, permanently. I'm sorry I said it in the way I did. Full marks for putting my foot in it but, not having done it before, it didn't come easy.' He stopped, and raised his glass to his lips, his fingers white around the bowl.

Liza watched him, weakness flooding her reasoning. Did he mean it? How desperately she wanted to believe him. So why couldn't she? She knew in an instant of sanity. Graham! He'd blocked her reasoning, was still blocking it even now. She was so terrified of that final rejection that she believed it was inevitable.

'Robert.' He put down his glass, waited for her to go on. She struggled inwardly, forced herself to move her lips. 'I'm scared,' she admitted in a hoarse whisper. 'I'm scared to love you.'

Slowly, very slowly, he reached across the table and took her hand, ran his thumb over the back of it. 'I know, and I'm scared too, terrified you'll refuse me. I love you, Liza.'

She grasped his hand. 'I love you too, Robert.' The weight lifted from her heart, the relief so immense she felt giddy.

'And you'll marry me?' he said softly, expectantly.

'We don't have to marry...' She stopped, looked in to his jet eyes and smiled. She was still fighting him, not wanting the full commitment for fear he would change his mind. But he wouldn't; she knew that deep in her heart. 'Yes, I'll marry you,' she breathed happily.

Later, when the motor boat had delivered them back to the jetty next to the flower barge, Robert took her in his arms. He kissed her so thoroughly and demandingly that she swayed with the depth of feeling that pushed every last doubt from her spinning senses.

When at last he released her he held her by her trembling shoulders and gazed deeply in to her misty green eyes. 'I vowed that when you finally agreed to marry me I wouldn't make love to you till you wore my ring, but——'

'But it seems you make an awful lot of vows just to break them,' Liza interrupted with a laugh. 'You vowed bachelorhood, and now look at you!' she teased.

'Now look at me,' he laughed back. 'Besotted.' He tightened her shawl around her as she shivered with cold and happiness. 'And impatient,' he added meaningfully. 'We can't get married on the spot...'

'And we can't make love on the spot either,' she giggled.

They both looked up at the hotel and without another word Robert took her hand; together they crossed the cobbled street and hurried in to the foyer, Robert's arm folded tightly around her as if never to let her go.

CHAPTER NINE

ROBERT and Liza returned the next day, and walked out of Heathrow airport unmolested.

'Amazing! When you want the media they are nowhere in sight,' Robert breathed jokingly. 'What better way to announce our engagement?'

'Don't even think about it!' Liza warned with a laugh. 'My parents have had enough shocks this week without reading in the gossip columns that their daughter is actually going to *marry* the infamous Robert Buchanan. I want to tell them myself.'

'Will they mind?'

'Mind my marrying a millionaire?' She grinned impishly. 'I'm sure they'll be overjoyed!'

'I knew it was my money you were after,' he teased. 'Remind me to change my will to leave all my money to Battersea Dogs' Home!'

Laughing together, they hurried across the concourse to where Carl was waiting.

'Good trip, Mr Buchanan, Miss Kay?'

Robert squeezed Liza's hand in the back of the car. 'Very productive, thank you, Carl. Another take-over accomplished; not without a struggle, though.'

'Congratulations, sir...' Liza nearly exploded at that. Carl couldn't possibly understand

Robert's double meaning but his reply was very apt. 'Sorry to be the bearer of bad news, but David Cassals said to call him immediately. The unions are giving trouble down at Essex, threatening strike action.'

'Damn!' Robert cursed and reached for the car phone.

It didn't sound good and Liza tensed for Robert.

'Sorry, darling, but I'll have to get down there immediately,' he said, slamming the phone down after speaking to David. 'We'll drop you home first of course.'

Home. Suddenly Liza remembered Graham, opened her mouth to tell Robert of his phone call, but the car phone bleeped and immediately Robert picked up the receiver again. It was the printing works and there was a long heated conversation, and Liza sat silent. She'd tell him about Graham when this crisis was over. He had enough to contend with at the moment.

'I'll call you later, darling,' Robert said as they pulled up outside Liza's town house. He leaned across and planted a kiss on her lips, and as the limousine pulled away Liza smiled and gave a resigned shrug of her shoulders, doubting she'd see much of him over the weekend.

Graham arrived at eight on the dot that evening and as Liza opened the door to him she knew that a chapter of her life was over; in fact she wondered what all the fuss had been about in the first place. Yes, she had loved him, a sort of love different from that she held in her heart for Robert, though. As she reached up and kissed her brother-in-law on the cheek their differences flashed across her mind—the difference in temperaments, the endless list of subjects they had disagreed on. How had she ever believed they could have married and been happy?

'Liza, you're looking marvellous. All that adverse publicity doesn't appear to have affected you at all.'

Liza laughed as she ran upstairs, Graham following. 'I don't suppose it will be the last,' she said mysteriously.

She told him over dinner, a frozen leg of lamb defrosted in the microwave and roasted with potatoes and vegetables.

'Robert has asked me to marry him,' she said, passing him the mint sauce.

Graham let out a low whistle, one of those aggravating habits of his that now she could accept. 'And you've agreed?' Liza nodded.

'I suppose I should have known by the radiance oozing from you,' he laughed. Then his brown eyes softened. 'I'm glad for you, Liza. Yvonne will be over the moon too. What about your parents?'

'Delighted. I called them as soon as I got back. They can't wait to meet him.' As always, her parents were there when she needed them.

'You know, it wouldn't have worked for us——' Graham started to say.

'I know that now,' Liza interrupted gently. 'I think your rejection clouded the real issue: that we just weren't compatible enough for marriage. You know how I hate to be thought wrong. I couldn't accept it, didn't until Robert, I suppose. And then of course there was sibling rivalry. I didn't realise that Yvonne really loved you. I just thought she wanted you because she's always wanted everything I had. Books and toys when we were kids, clothes and make-up in our teens.'

Graham laughed. 'She's grown up a lot since our marriage. I don't think you'll have any trouble from her any more.'

'I hope not; I wouldn't want her to make a play for Robert,' Liza said light-heartedly. How easily she could joke about such things now, safe in the knowledge that Robert's love for her was strong and true.

'Much as I love my wife, I think Robert Buchanan might be out of her league. You're right for him, Liza. I don't know the man, of course, but I'd assume he's pretty demanding, and you can match him.'

Liza afforded herself an inner smile of reflection. Yes, she could match him; last night in the lovely Hotel Delft overlooking the canal had proved that! Though she doubted Graham was referring to the intimate side of her and Robert's relationship.

'Tell me about your latest book, Graham. I'm dying to hear all about it.'

They spent a pleasant and relaxing evening together. Yvonne phoned and Liza talked with her for a long while, about the cottage and the expected baby, and then Graham took over, impatient to know how his wife was coping without him. They truly loved each other, and the thought that at last they were going to be a united family was so pleasing to Liza that she thought her happiness couldn't be more complete.

Graham left far too late, laughing that he'd never get up the next morning to catch his train back to Wales.

Liza gave him a brotherly peck on the cheek at the front door and when she closed it after him she realised just how exhausted she was.

She slept late the next morning, rose after eleven, and switched on the answerphone Robert had insisted on installing for her when she joined Magnum. There were no messages and, disappointed that Robert hadn't called, she moped around the house, half-heartedly looking for jobs to occupy herself with.

By mid-afternoon she was getting anxious; by late afternoon, frantic. She called the print works only to learn that Robert was in a meeting with the union representatives and couldn't be disturbed. She felt only marginally better, and vowed not to act the typical clinging female and keep pestering him with phone calls. He was obviously up to his neck in a dispute.

Sunday was one of the longest days of her life. Robert still hadn't called and, not wanting to miss

him in case he did, she decided against visiting
her parents, and spent the day viciously cleaning
the house from top to bottom, tensing every time
she heard the slightest sound, fully expecting
Robert to phone or come to the house.

On her way to work Monday morning she had
calmed herself enough to reason that this was
what life would be like with Robert Buchanan.
He ran a powerful organisation and these
company eruptions were more than likely a way
of life for him, and would be hers too once they
were married. She'd missed him though, achingly
so.

Her staff were all at their consoles when Liza
clipped across the office in her high heels. She
wondered how they would react when they heard
the news that she and Robert were going to be
married. She called out a cheery good morning
as she went. She frowned slightly at the lack-
lustre response. That atmosphere again; no doubt
they'd heard of the dispute down at the print
works and were anxious to know how it would
affect them. Hopefully Robert would be able to
reassure them when he arrived. He wasn't in yet;
she'd seen no sign of his car, which was usually
parked out front, Carl always at the ready to
whisk him away to some meeting or other.

'David,' she called as she was about to step
into her office.

David Cassals strode across the floor to her,
that perpetual grin on his face.

'What's happening with the dispute?' Liza asked.

'All over. Storm in a teacup. They went back to work yesterday afternoon,' he told her. His bleeper sounded and he excused himself to the nearest phone, and with a frown Liza stepped into her office.

Why hadn't Robert called to tell her? He must have been too exhausted, she reasoned, though the thought didn't settle her.

'Good morning, Julia,' she breezed, forcing a smile and flinging her suede jacket over the back of a chair.

Julia, standing by the window, gazing out over the green below, jumped as if she'd been shot. She turned, and Liza was just about to comment on her pale appearance when the door was flung open.

'Out!' roared Robert, his fearful command directed at Julia, who moved so fast she nearly fell over herself to get to the door.

'Robert, what's wrong?' Liza blurted. She'd never seen him so furious. Gauntness showed through the flush of anger on his face, though, and in that split second before his anger capitulated into near violence she thought the worst had happened and the strike had erupted again, and Magnum's future was about to be terminated.

'You dare to show your face in here?' he roared, stepping towards her so violently she steeled herself back against her desk.

'What...what do you mean?' Her senses spun wildly. Surely he didn't think because they were going to be married she wouldn't turn up....? No, this was something else. Her pulse rate increased dangerously.

'Don't look so astounded. You know damn well what I mean! You've made a fool of me, and no one does that! Not even the likes of you!'

'Robert!' she almost screamed, her eyes wide with terror. 'What's happened?'

With a muted roar he slammed his fist down on her desk. 'Don't play the innocent with me...' He stopped suddenly, and stared at her speechless for a second before stinging viciously at her, 'It worked, Liza. Very clever, but I wonder if now that you have him back he realises what a conniving, devious mistress he's landed himself with. I hope you both think that breaking up a marriage is worth it!'

'Break...breaking up a marriage?' she floundered. Her face went white. 'Graham, you mean Graham?'

Robert's eyes were wild with fury. 'Who else? No sooner is my back turned and he's there, back in your life, or maybe he's never been out of it. You arranged the Press helicopter, trying to make him jealous——'

'Robert!' Liza screeched, appalled at the suggestion. 'I didn't...I wouldn't——'

'Wouldn't you? I think you're capable of anything. You agreed to marry me and the very next night you're shacked up with him again. I've lived twenty-four hours with this,' he grated, 'strikes, take-overs—nothing compares to what you've done to me...'

'Oh, God, no!' she cried, turning away from him and covering her face with her hands. 'How did you...?'

How did he know? It was obvious, wasn't it? He wasn't furious for nothing. The world knew. She turned slowly, faced his fury with pain in her heart.

'The papers?' she breathed hopelessly.

He held her gaze, still angry. 'Of course, I was forgetting—you don't read that sort of paper, do you?' he lanced sarcastically. 'Well, on your way out of my life and Magnum's I suggest you pick up the weekend's tabloids and indulge yourself. It didn't make pleasant reading for me, but no doubt you'll be delighted with the outcome.' With that he turned and powered out of her office.

Shaking with shock, Liza stood where she was, trying to think, to clear the fuzz from her brain. What on earth had happened? Seconds later she moved jerkily, lifted her jacket and her bag from the chair and walked out of the office. She was unaware of the looks, the speculation, the possibility that Robert's fury could have been overheard. All she was aware of was the feverish need to get away.

Outside in the cool fresh air, she slipped on her jacket, hailed a taxi, the ritual shaking some life back into her.

She asked the taxi driver to stop at her local newsagent, where she bought all the weekend papers they had left over. She stepped back into the taxi, fighting the urge to skim through them. She needed the sanctity of a closed door between her and the world before she dared look.

Once inside her own home she tore through them, her heart beating so fast she felt sick. With a terrible despair she burst into tears when she saw the photo of her kissing Graham goodbye at two in the morning on her doorstep. Had it been that late? she questioned crazily. Did it damn well matter what time it was? The damage was done at whatever hour! She felt ill and weak with anger as she read the filth and the lies: 'Robert Buchanan's latest mistress, entertaining the writer Graham Bond as soon as the publishing magnate's back was turned.' Poor Graham, poor Yvonne and, more than anything, poor Robert.

The tears gave way to fury, directed at herself, punishing herself for being so complacent. Lulled into a false sense of security by the lack of interest shown by the Press while they were in Holland, she hadn't thought...hadn't imagined for a second that they hadn't let up. Someone had seen her return with Robert and later Graham arriving for dinner. And, not satisfied with that, they had waited for him to go, noting the hour, and snapped that brotherly kiss as she'd bid him goodbye. It couldn't be worse, the evidence so damning she understood Robert's rage.

Liza curled tightly on the sofa with the papers crumpled beside her. What could she do? Robert was convinced it was all true, and how could she convince him it wasn't?

The phone rang and she leapt to it. 'Yvonne? Yvonne, what can I say?' she blurted, more tears springing to her eyes. Her sister didn't deserve this.

'Liza, listen to me. Don't cry. It's OK. We understand...' Her sister's voice broke. 'We...we all know it's not true. I spoke to Mummy this morning. She didn't know anything about it. I said I was going to call you and she said she'll come over to see you——'

'No, I don't want that...I can't see anyone, Yvonne.' Liza rubbed viciously at her eyes. 'Call her back and tell her not to come...I'm...I'm all right, just need some time to think.'

'What are you going to do? I mean you're not going to let them get away with it, are you?'

'What can I do?' Liza wailed. 'You can't fight the media!' She let out a ragged sigh of defeat. 'The family knows it's a pack of lies. We'll get over it, but...but Robert...' The anxiety in her voice said it all.

'He believes it!' Yvonne was aghast. 'But how could he? He loves you——'

'Obviously not enough!' Liza bit out dejectedly. That was the worst hurt of all, knowing that Robert believed everything he'd read, wasn't prepared to hear her side of the story. She took a deep breath. 'He thinks there isn't smoke without fire, I suppose.'

'And you're going to go on letting him believe that?' Her sister suddenly sounded angry. 'Listen to me, Liza. You love him, don't you? Well, fight for him!' There was a pause as Yvonne gathered her strength. 'I've never told you this before, but I fought for Graham,' she admitted hoarsely. 'I know what I did was bad, but I loved him, Liza, wanted him badly enough to take him from my own sister. I'm not proud of it, not one bit, but you don't think of that when you love someone so much. You didn't fight for Graham, did you?'

The question confused Liza's already over-taxed brain. 'What do you mean?'

'You let me take him from you, gave up without a fight because deep down you didn't care enough. Is that how you feel about Robert? You don't care enough to fight for him?'

Liza rubbed her fingers across her damp forehead. Her little sister, suddenly so mature that she knew the answers to everything. How true: she'd let Graham slide out of her life because she hadn't cared enough. Her love for Robert was different. There was no life without him.

Liza smiled through her tears. 'You're right,' she husked. 'I love Robert too much to give in.'

Yvonne let out a sigh of relief. 'Go for it, Liza.'

Go for it, Liza mused after she had put the receiver down. And suppose Robert didn't go for it, refused to hear her out? Negative thinking.

Determinedly she phoned for a cab, washed her face and re-applied her make-up while she waited. She'd have to go to him at Magnum, doubting that he would agree to come to her in his present frame of mind. Besides, she had other business at Magnum. Something that had been nagging deep inside her as she had read the papers, something that needed to be sorted out before she tackled Robert.

'Oh...oh...you're back,' Julia hesitantly said as she stepped out of her office into Liza's.

'Yes, I'm back,' Liza clipped. She folded her arms across her chest, stood by the window and looked at her assistant, wondering why she hadn't acted on her intuition before. When Robert had pointed out that she and Nigel were having an affair she had defended them both, ignoring the warning apprehension she had felt then. She doubted if Nigel had anything to do with this. Men weren't like that.

'I think you have something to say to me,' Liza began.

'I...I don't know what you mean.' Julia flushed darkly as she stood by her door, gripping it tightly.

'You do. There is guilt written all over your face. I'll help you, shall I? You suspected Robert and I were having an affair and thought the media might be interested in a bit of scandal. You no doubt overheard Robert saying we would be working from his home that weekend. And I suspect that you misconstrued the telephone conversation with my brother-in-law——'

'Your brother-in-law!' Julia gasped, her face blanching.

'Yes, Graham Bond is married to my sister,' Liza told her evenly, waiting for it to sink in before she went on. 'Do you realise the damage you've done, to me and my family?'

Hesitantly Julia came towards her and stopped by Liza's desk. 'I didn't mean anything, Liza. Honestly. I just thought you and Robert were having a bit of a fling. They paid me a lot of money the first time and...and offered more. You were talking to Robert when I went out of the office and when I came back I thought you were still talking to him, arranging to have dinner with him at your home Friday night.'

'I was arranging to see my brother-in-law, not Robert. But it makes no difference whom I was seeing. You did a wicked thing.' Her green eyes darkened and narrowed. 'Why, Julia? Why did you do it?'

Julia's whole body slackened weakly. She lowered her eyes in shame. 'Money,' she confessed in a weak whisper. 'I wanted more money. Nigel and I——'

'Did he know about this?'

Julia shook her head. 'No. I did it on my own. Got in touch with the Press myself. We wanted to go on this holiday together but Nigel couldn't afford to pay for us both. I was afraid of losing him, afraid he might go with one of the other girls.'

'I thought you were close.'

Julia shook her head dismally. 'We were at first, then he seemed to cool a bit, especially after you bawled him out for not reaching his targets. I suppose I was angry with you for that as well.'

'Revenge as well as money,' Liza sighed. What women did for love! 'I'll have to let you go,' she said stoically. She felt sorry for her in a way, but there was no excuse for what she had done. 'I can never trust you again. You realise that, don't you, Julia?'

'Trust me?' Julia gasped incredulously. 'Let me go? You don't work here any more! Robert sacked you; everyone's saying he sacked you! You can't throw me out!'

'I can and I will...'

The door opened and Robert Buchanan walked in, his eyes darkening at the sight of Liza. 'What the hell's going on here?'

'I was just firing Julia,' Liza stated flatly, though her heart was leaping so wildly inside her she was sure they must hear it pounding against her ribcage. 'I won't bore you with the details why,' she directed at Robert, 'unless of course Julia wants to tell you herself, but I doubt after hearing that we are going to be married, that she'll bother!'

The silence that followed filled the room to bursting point. Julia was the first to react; with a small sob of frustration she flew into her own office and came out with her coat and bag.

'Julia,' Liza's cool voice halted her at the door, 'don't bother trying to get more money from your newspaper friends for that piece of information. Robert is quite capable of announcing his own wedding plans, thank you.'

The door slammed so hard after her that Liza flinched. She looked at Robert, terrified now that she had overstepped herself, so afraid that she plopped down at her desk before her legs gave in.

Robert found his voice at last. She'd stunned him into silence, and that was a state she had never seen him in before. It was almost frightening.

'Explain,' was all he could muster.

'Where do you want me to begin?' she asked him quietly.

He raised his hand to the door. 'That, for starters.'

Coolly and calmly Liza told him everything. How it was Julia who'd informed the Press. The conversation on the phone she had misinterpreted, thinking she was arranging to dine with Robert instead of her brother-in-law.

'And you came back to sack her?' Robert asked coldly when she had concluded.

For a moment her heart sank to the pit of her stomach. He wasn't going to listen, his tone told her he couldn't care less about Julia and even less about her coming back to Magnum's offices.

'One of the reasons. Another was to say I love you, and the other to tell you what a bastard you are!' She held his gaze of disbelief with one of iron resolve. She was going to have her say whatever he thought.

'You have the nerve to make me out the guilty party!' he exploded in exasperation. 'I don't care a damn what Julia did; it doesn't alter the fact that you had your ex-lover at your house half the night and the world witnessed it.'

'I had my *brother-in-law* in my house half the night!' Liza flamed back. Had she thought this was going to be easy? 'But that really isn't the problem, is it? The truth is, you think the world is laughing at you. The mighty Robert Buchanan, losing face! That is more important than reasoning out my feelings for you. Unbelievable, isn't it? The publicity you so readily accept has spat in your face, and you can't take that, can you?'

'Could you?' he thundered back, a pulse jerking so hard at his jawline Liza thought it was all hopeless.

'I've taken it. I had to go through the turmoil of reading you were practically married off to Lady Victoria——'

'That was before us——'

'It wasn't!' Liza cut back. 'Not for me it wasn't. I loved you then; when I really come to think about it I suppose I fell in love with you from the moment you and your arrogance stepped into my *Leisure Days* office. But I coped with that, believed you when you said there was nothing between you. I trusted you. But you don't trust me, do you? Even after the floods and Amsterdam you still believed that I wanted Graham back, believed that I had used you and arranged that stunt with the helicopter to get him back.'

Robert raked a hand through his hair, turned away from her and stood by the window. 'What was I supposed to think?' he grated, still angry.

Still hurt, Liza realised with a sickening tightening of her stomach muscles. She was losing him. His pride and that fearful arrogance of his could never be broken down.

'I don't know what you were supposed to think,' she murmured. 'It's a silly question anyway.' She drew a long breath. 'Graham phoned me and said he was coming down to town and offered his support over the flood story. I thought nothing of asking him over for a meal. It was no secret. Yvonne phoned that evening; we resolved our differences. They were both delighted about you and me. I...I know he was my lover once, but that's past now. He's married to my sister, he's family, and you'll be family too if you stop being unreasonable and believe that I love you and only you.'

'Nevertheless you chose not to tell me about it,' he grated bitterly without looking at her.

'I didn't *choose* not to. I honestly forgot the arrangement. Only remembered when we were in the car coming back from the airport and you were on the phone. I didn't want to bring our personal life up when you had a strike on your hands.'

He didn't believe her—she could tell by the determined set of his shoulders. Liza bit her lip, walked over to him, hesitantly placed her hand on his arm and said quietly, 'You know, my sister raised a very valid point when she called me this morning. She said I'd let go of Graham easily because I didn't care enough for him. She was right. I let him go because my feelings weren't deep enough. I didn't put up a fight. I am now. I'm fighting for *you*, Robert. That's why I came back here. To tell you I love you and want to be with you for the rest of our lives, but . . . but only if you want me.' The tears came then, filled her wide green eyes and threatened to spill at any moment.

He turned slowly from the window, and faced her. She saw no softness in his drawn features. She had failed, hopelessly. Misjudged the depth of his feelings for her. With a small cry torn from her heart she turned away.

He reached for her, swung her back to him and gripped her shoulders so fiercely that she jerked her head up and cried out.

'Do you realise what you've nearly done to me?' he husked bitterly.

'Nearly?' she croaked, trembling in his grip.

'Yes, nearly. You came close to destroying me.' Suddenly he lurched her against him, a deep shudder powering through him. 'I was so enraged when I read the papers that I wanted to kill. I've never experienced jealousy before. Even trying to reason that you did love me didn't help. I couldn't believe that you'd deceived me, and yet there was the evidence, in black and white and for all the world to see. It was worse than walking into that bedroom and thinking you were crushed under that tree. I would have been devastated by your death, but thinking you still loved Graham was somehow worse. I'm more than in love with you, Liza. You're an obsession I can't live without. Don't you realise that?'

She clung to him then, half laughing, half crying with happiness. His arms held her strongly, unrelentingly.

'Why are you still so angry with me, then?' she sobbed against his shirt.

'It's part of my love for you, the pain and the hurt. I've never loved before, didn't realise it would be so hard. I'm still battling with myself, but you're winning. Darling, I'm sorry for what I thought, furious with myself for not having faith in you.' Slowly he lifted her tear-stained face to his, kissed her freckles, and gently manoeuvred her mouth to his. His lips trembled against hers, unsure at first, then her warmth and her deep love coaxed him on. With an impassioned groan he gave himself up in surrender, his kiss all she needed to tell her her fight had not been in vain.

When at last he drew away from her she was left weak and senseless. 'For two reluctant lovers we aren't doing so bad, are we?' he murmured into her flame hair. 'Let's get married now; within the hour if that's possible.'

She looked up at him, the love shining in her bright green eyes. Slowly she shook her head. 'We can't,' she laughed up at him. 'It wouldn't be fair to our public.' She raised a hand and smoothed the frown from his brow. 'We're going to have a huge wedding and invite every reporter and photographer, and then perhaps they'll leave us in peace. Forever after.'

Robert kissed her eyelids. 'First we'll get them to print a retraction on that latest gossip; only then will I invite them to a champagne reception. And if ever they publish anything about our marriage heading for disaster, I'll——'

'Buy them out?' Liza interrupted with a grin.

He shook his head with a gleam in his eye. 'No, I'll forget it, and so will you, because nothing can touch us from now on. Nothing in the world is going to shake this marriage, my reluctant mistress, nothing in this world or the next.'

'Whatever you say, my darling,' she murmured against his mouth as it came down to seal their love for evermore.

YOU CAN AFFORD THAT HOLIDAY!

Great savings can be made when you book your next holiday – whether you want to go skiing, take a luxury cruise, or lie in the Mediterranean sun – the Holiday Club offers you the chance to receive **FREE HOLIDAY SPENDING MONEY** worth up to 10% of the cost of your holiday!

All you have to do is choose a holiday from one of the major holiday companies including Thomson, Cosmos, Horizon, Cunard, Kuoni, Jetsave and many more.

Just call us* and ask if the holiday company you wish to book with is included.

HOW MUCH SPENDING MONEY WILL I RECEIVE?

The amount you receive is based on the basic price of your holiday. Add up the total cost for all holiday-makers listed on your booking form – excluding surcharges, supplements, insurance, car hire or special excursions where these are not included in the basic cost, and after any special reductions which may be offered on the holiday – then compare the total with the price bands below:-

YOUR TOTAL BASIC HOLIDAY PRICE FOR ALL PASSENGERS	HOLIDAY SPENDING MONEY
200 449	20
450 649	30
650 849	40
850 1099	60
1100 1499	80
1500 1999	100 ...
... 8500 or more	500

FREE

Having paid the balance of your holiday 10 weeks prior to travelling, your **FREE HOLIDAY SPENDING MONEY** will be sent to you with your tickets in the form of a cheque from the Holiday Club approximately 7-10 days before departure.

We reserve the right to decline any booking at our discretion. All holidays are subject to availability and the terms and conditions of the tour operators.

HOW TO BOOK

1. CHOOSE YOUR HOLIDAY from one of the major holiday companies brochures, making a note of the flight and hotel codes.

2. PHONE IT THROUGH* with your credit card details for the deposit and insurance premium, or full payment if within 10 weeks of departure and quote P&M Ref: H&C/MBC185. Your holiday must be booked with the Holiday Club before 30.6.92 and taken before 31.12.93.

3. SEND THE BOOKING FORM from the brochure to the address above, marking the top right hand corner of the booking form with P&M Ref: H&C/MBC185.

If you prefer to book by post or wish to pay the deposit by cheque, omit stage 2 and simply mail your booking to us. We will contact you if your holiday is not available.

Send to: The Holiday Club
P O Box 155 Leicester LE1 9GZ
* Tel No. (0533) 513377
Mon – Fri 9 am – 8 pm, Sat 9 am – 4 pm
Sun and Bank Holidays 10 am – 4 pm

CONDITIONS OF OFFER

Most people like to take out holiday insurance to cover for loss of possessions or injury. It is a condition of the offer that Page & Moy will arrange suitable insurance for you – further details are available on request. In order to provide comprehensive cover insurance will become payable upon confirmation of your holiday. The insurance premium is not refundable on cancellation.

Free Holiday Spending Money is not payable if travel on the holiday does not take place.

The Holiday Club is run by Page & Moy Ltd, Britain's largest single location travel agency and a long standing member of ABTA.

N.B. Any contractual arrangements are between yourselves and the tour operators not Mills & Boon Ltd.

ABTA 99529 Page & Moy Ltd Reg No. 1151142

WIN A LUXURY CRUISE

TO THE MEDITERRANEAN AND BLACK SEA

Last month we told you all about the fabulous cruise you could win just by entering our competition and sending in two tokens from November and December Romances.

For the lucky winner the popular cruise ship the Kareliya will be a floating hotel visiting eight exciting ports of call, including Lisbon, Athens and Istanbul.

For your chance to win this fabulous cruise for two people just answer these three questions and the tie-breaker which follows:

1. Which country is renowned for its delicious port? ....

2. Which volcano is situated on the island of Sicily? ....

3. Which Turkish city sits at the mouth of the Bosphorus? ....

Tie-Breaker. Tell us in no more than 15 words which romantic partner you would like to take on a cruise with you and why ....

....

....

Name: ....

Address:...

....Postcode:......................................

Are you a Reader Service subscriber?　　Yes ☐　　No ☐

You may be mailed with offers from other reputable companies as a result of this entry. If you do not wish to receive such information please tick this box ☐.

Send your entry, together with two tokens, a red one from November and a blue one from December Romances by 31st January 1992 to:

Holiday Competition　Mills & Boon Reader Service
P.O. Box 236　Thornton Road　Croydon　Surrey　CR9 3RU

Next month's Romances

Each month, you can choose from a world of variety in romance with Mills & Boon. These are the new titles to look out for next month.

DESPERATE MEASURES Sara Craven

STRANGER FROM THE PAST Penny Jordan

FATED ATTRACTION Carole Mortimer

A KIND OF MAGIC Betty Neels

A CANDLE FOR THE DEVIL Susanne McCarthy

TORRID CONFLICT Angela Wells

LAST SUMMER'S GIRL Elizabeth Barnes

DESERT DESTINY Sarah Holland

THE CORSICAN GAMBIT Sandra Marton

GAMES FOR SOPHISTICATES Diana Hamilton

SUBSTITUTE HUSBAND Margaret Callaghan

MIRROR IMAGE Melinda Cross

LOVE BY DESIGN Rosalie Ash

IN PURSUIT OF LOVE Jayne Bauling

NO LAST SONG Ann Charlton

STARSIGN

ENIGMA MAN Nicola West

Available from Boots, Martins, John Menzies, W.H. Smith, most supermarkets and other paperback stockists.

Also available from Mills and Boon Reader Service, P.O. Box 236, Thornton Road, Croydon, Surrey CR9 3RU.